As a child Suzy wanted to be Georg[e]
actually more like Anne. Neil prob[ably]

This book began fifteen years [ago]
round the island of Sark, which reminded them of the so-phisticated fictional world of Kirrin Island, with its endless and endlessly repeated summer holidays. They began to speculate what life might be like for childhood characters if they had grown up and had to face the modern world. 1979 seemed a pivotal year.

In 1979, they were both at University. Suzy, after a few jobs as a high-kicking chorus girl, a seaside hotel nanny and (very briefly) a bank clerk, settled on teaching. This was really so she could read lots of stories to her class, first in Tower Hamlets (London) then in Frome (Somerset). Neil was about to leave Oxbridge academia to cram law in a polytechnic, and worked for many years in criminal and mental health law. They have two grown up children.

The first thing anyone said on hearing they were writing a book together was and you're still married? They are, and live in Frome.

Neil and Suzy Howlett

SilverWood

Published in 2017 by Kirrin Enterprises Ltd

ISBN 978-1-9998120-0-3 (paperback)
ISBN 978-1-9998120-1-0 (ebook)

British Library Cataloguing in Publication Data
A CIP catalogue record for this book is available from the British Library

Page design and typesetting by SilverWood Books
Printed on responsibly sourced paper

To our children, George and Lucy, and libraries everywhere

Contents

1

Anne is Excited!

Anne Stonehouse gave the leaves of her spider plant a last wipe – quite a fiddle, but definitely worth it – and arranged it back in the macramé pot holder with satisfaction. So many lovely babies! And all just the image of their mother plant which held them so tidily, all properly attached on good, strong stems! She hummed along to the radio. 'Happy to be on an island in the sun…' Gosh, how apt! And what a glorious day! So important for the first day of the hols.

Rules change all the time, of course, but Anne didn't know that. Her J-Cloth was as blue as the sky visible through the window. True, there were clouds to the west, but only small ones, and the conservatories of Wimbledon didn't care. They gleamed on regardless. A movement, reflected in the window glass, made her turn round. Oh dear!

"No, darling, it's been on the floor. It's picked up germs. You can't possibly pack it now!" Jonny was terribly slow at grasping the most basic rules of hygiene. With a little sigh, Anne took the carefully made egg and tomato sandwich and dropped it into the waste bin. Jonny blinked hard at her and squeezed the secret, plastic Jaws shark in his pocket.

Anne's kitchen gave her pleasure. The country look was very

much cosier than the garish colours that lots of people seemed to like. She'd *looked* at the rather go-ahead Habitat catalogues with her friend Hilary when she had been planning her kitchen. Although the new mixer taps and the orange Formica surfaces had looked so fresh in the photographs they would be, Anne thought, a bit startling to come down to in the morning. She was sure that Hilary now agreed with her that the Pine Farmhouse range was much lovelier. Rupert was always very good about that, at least; letting her make decisions around the house, and paying for them.

Anne had written neatly on a small notepad: *No milk, please, until Tuesday.* She tore it off and looked up dreamily. Packing for the great family reunion on Kirrin Island had to be right. Julie and Jonny would so enjoy a picnic the way she and the others used to, and eleven was a lovely age! Her eyes shone at the memory. Of course, in those days Joan had packed up the most marvellous baskets for them, in the warmth of Aunt Fanny's kitchen. It was this kitchen, Anne suddenly realised, that she had tried hard to emulate, though with hygienic surfaces and proper refrigeration.

Anne had made a careful list for Mrs. Finniston, telling her what to include in the hamper. No visit to Kirrin could possibly be complete without a picnic, especially as Anne hadn't seen the place for so many years, and the twins had never been at all! Her instructions to Mrs. Finniston had been firm but, of course, respectful. Anne's training as a counsellor saw to that. The hard-boiled eggs must be Lion stamped and the bread nice and soft. Waitrose even had plums out of season, and they would be a super treat. Mrs. F. had bottled some homemade ginger beer, although Anne noticed it did look terribly similar to the Schweppes one Rupert had with his nightly whisky.

Nevertheless, Anne had drawn the line at cold tongue. She

shuddered a little. They used to eat it, tins and tins of the stuff, in sandwiches, sliced up with ham, and even for breakfast. But was it quite nice? And would her children eat it, or would they make rebellious 'yucky' faces at her? Parma ham would be far more suitable.

Julie, who was perched on a kitchen chair, shut her book and wrinkled her nose at the glowing schoolgirls on the cover. They were having some sort of romp with a hairbrush and a tennis racquet, and looked annoyingly chummy. The twins had been keeping up a campaign to go to the McDonald's on the bypass near Kirrin. Julie had found it on the directions included with Uncle Julian's invitation. She opened her mouth to try again.

"Mummy, *why* can't we go to McDonald's? *Loads* of our friends have been to a McDonald's. Everyone talks about it. They do these special chips called French Fries in a little box thingie, and they're all thin. You *never* let me…never. Daddy says you're uptight about it. He says…"

"*For mash get Smash,*" put in Jonny.

Anne looked a little forlorn.

"Darling, you know Daddy can't come; you know he is much too busy with his clever work. And the food in those places! All that horrid grease, and you don't know how it's prepared." She shivered. "Now, time to fetch your violin. You can't afford to miss any practice with Grade II coming up. Jonny, you bring your anorak and your spellings, please, there's plenty of room in the car. Isn't it kind of Daddy to let us use the car for a whole weekend away! He didn't seem to mind very much." She turned her attention back to packing; antiseptic moist towelettes, insect repellent spray, first-aid kit, Tupperware container of scouring powder (the baths might not be *quite* as they should be), bottles of asthma drops for Jonny. Surely there was something else?

11

"*Oooh, Betty!*" Jonny simpered. "*The cat's done a whoopsie in my beret!*"

Anne frowned for a moment. Where on earth did Jonny pick up these things? She was so careful to monitor her children's television viewing. She put it out of her mind and sighed dreamily again. Kirrin Castle! Darling Julian would be there, and good old Dick. George would join them with her old dog Gary. Ah yes, Gary. That was the other thing on Anne's list – the handy plastic shovel especially designed for clearing up after man's (or woman's) best friend – a little present for George. George, Anne remembered, was rather unobservant when it came to Gary's personal habits. Oh dear; Anne did hope George wouldn't be *difficult* these holidays.

2

Dick is Frustrated

Dick scuffled up the dark stairs, found the keyhole after a few tries, opened the lock and stumbled through the door into his flat. He stopped, leaning over and breathing heavily as he turned on the light.

"Come one, old chap," he told himself, as he snapped on the switch and nearly tripped over a misplaced pile of laundry. He thought about going to the kitchenette, but decided to collapse on the settee. He flung his jacket onto the floor and focused with some effort on the blank TV screen.

"What's on?" he asked the settee, but decided that whatever it was, the effort of getting up again to press the button wasn't worth it. He waved his hand towards the screen but accepted he didn't possess the magic power of controlling it from a distance. The vinyl seat cushion squeaked under him. Dick was left with his own thoughts.

"Next time, if I don't catch them in the first fifty yards I'm giving up," he told the poster of the tennis girl scratching her bottom. "I'll make sure I'm a lot closer before I start running." He looked down at his stomach, which was not hard to miss these days, and sighed. He was forty-one, he wasn't ever going to outrun Daley Thompson, and neither could he match up to his moustache, though he had tried. How had it come to this?

And why did young men object so often when you stopped them on 'sus'? He was generally pretty polite and friendly about it, compared to most of his colleagues. And it was in their own interests if he stopped them before they committed a crime, as they probably would.

Dick thought of himself as a decent and open-minded policeman. These days he didn't judge people on whether their shoes were cleaned and polished. He didn't agree with his fellows who thought that just because someone was banged up they were also banged to rights, even when their provocative smart-alec briefs turned up and started asking for proof. Nor would Dick join his friends in 'making sure' that the truly guilty were convicted. It created too much paperwork explaining where the stuff from the evidence store had gone, and anyway it was wrong; planting evidence was not on and he hadn't joined the police for that. He sighed again. His arrest rate was not impressive and sometimes trying to do the right thing was really hard.

It wasn't difficult to justify stopping someone. He had recently read *Signs of Crime,* that most interesting handbook for new bobbies on the beat, which told him that one person in a car was suspicious, two was more suspicious, and three provoca-tively so. He'd been told to watch out for any person who seemed nervous of him, as well as those who were friendly or fawningly servile. And, of course, there were the ones who adopted a bold approach by walking up to him and asking for the correct time. By the end of the book Dick could have found good reason to stop the Archbishop of Canterbury. Come to think of it, if he'd seen someone dressed like the Archbishop of Canterbury on the Railton Road he probably would have stopped him. "Excuse me, Your Grace, would you mind putting that big stick down while you empty your pockets for me?"

Dick believed there had to be a better way. He hoped his polite, un-confrontational manner diffused tension; some of his colleagues seemed to provoke trouble, getting their arrest rate up that way. They were not deliberately racist, he reckoned, despite the talk of *bongo bongo land*. Dick was a bit worried about the National Front members of the Met, especially when they wore their badges on patrol, but they were just a few bad apples, surely, and even they didn't actually want to provoke a riot.

There was another thing.

"That's the last time I go out drinking with the lads from the Special Patrol Group, especially not on fizzy lager." He burped, pardoned himself politely, and stared miserably at a cushion.

Dick wished he had that easy sense of belonging he had seen among some of his colleagues. Not that he was actually disliked – he wasn't shunned in the canteen – but he was pretty sure there was a bit of mockery going on. Not for the first time he wondered if it might have something to do with his unusual past. Although he had mentioned it once or twice with his superiors, he'd kept quiet about his childhood activities in the station. His background was not the sort of thing the PCs in the canteen would appreciate. He'd tried to lose his public-school accent and acquire some Estuary English, and swear a bit, but he supposed it wasn't that convincing. His hair was as long as he could get away with as a serving policemen, but that wasn't convincing either. A policeman's lot is not a happy one.

And the ladies. Women. Females. He couldn't quite remember what he was supposed to call them, but he knew *bird* wasn't the word to use when you were actually talking to one. Dick thought lots of them were lovely. He would have liked to get to know them properly, but in uniform they just weren't quite right. He tried to puzzle it out. They didn't *do* anything wrong.

They were efficient and nicely turned out, with neat notebooks and knowing looks. There were a few who behaved like blokes – heavy drinkers who knew how to swear – but they embarrassed him. Dick missed the easy relationship he used to have with his sister Anne and cousin George. They were friends, they were plucky, and when they were in a tight corner it hadn't mattered that they had been girls.

He hauled himself off the settee and flicked on the TV switch. There they were – Bodie and Doyle – the perfect team – The Professionals. How did Bodie always manage a witty comment for every occasion? And still make his arrests work? And Doyle even managed to find love and romance as he did it all.

"Dick, old chap," he said to himself, settling back onto the settee, "you're just not very good at this." Women in uniform, when it came to the nitty-gritty, just hadn't worked for him. Women out of uniform were rather a mystery, too. When it came to the ladies outside the Force he tended not to tell them he was a policeman anymore. When they found out he wasn't in The Sweeney they seemed to lose interest.

Once, to be a policeman was a fine thing, or would be if you got a bit of promotion. Dick had always dreamed of respect in a Superintendent's Office, or as a D.I. He had joined up to continue what had seemed so easy and natural – the thwarting of criminals and the prevailing of what was honest and right. His childhood credentials should surely have counted for something. He had form, dammit, and in a good way. But things in the Force worked differently and, fifteen years on, it hadn't happened.

He got up from the settee and stretched. Bodie was revving up the Capri and screeching off round a corner. Dick might not be the most active person when it came to running around, but he felt restless nevertheless. He looked through the window to the car park below. His own Capri was there, all ready for a bit of adventure. Dagenham's finest, it looked good, with its eight-track music player and reclining front seats. It might not be as fast as the motorway cops in their Ford Granadas but it could beat an Allegro away from the lights any day. But the Capri hadn't made an impression on anyone yet. It wasn't as if he was expecting Juliet Bravo. Just a good-looking girl. Or maybe not even that good looking. Just a *nice* one.

He shut the curtains and sighed yet again, plonking himself back on the cushions. No, he lamented, nobody loves a policeman. Not even his own brother and sister that much. Of course, they were both married, or in Julian's case, had been. He hadn't seen his brother since one of Anne's Christmas Drinks evenings a couple of years ago and even then, Julian had made his excuses and left early to go to something presumably more important. Anne had looked woebegone, he remembered.

As for his cousin George – well George had always been wild and *offbeat*, as it was called these days. When he had joined the Force she had sent a rather nasty note about going over to the dark side. He had been surprised at first, and hurt. They'd always been such a help to the police, and he had assumed they were all in agreement about what a fine bunch of fellows they were. Anne had tried to set up some kind of lunch party to congratulate him, but that hadn't really worked, either. In the end, Julian had been too busy to attend and George had stayed for about ten minutes, tried to talk him into resigning, and then stomped off. She'd always been one for extreme changes of mood and although she hadn't spoken to him in years Dick was pretty sure she had shouted at him at least once. He'd been in the thin blue line at a demonstration and she had looked the part in baggy dungarees. He couldn't remember now which demo it was. CND? Save The Whale? They were all confusingly similar, and the protesters all rather unkempt. *Something or other! Out, Out, Out!* they always chanted. She hadn't seen him, as far as he knew, and so he'd moved to the rear, claiming a twisted ankle. He hadn't fancied getting the sharp end of her tongue at close quarters, or a bash on the head with her placard. And she'd had a nasty looking dog with her.

Anne did invite him to Sunday lunch once a month, and Anne's roast potatoes were worth the journey to Wimbledon, but the conversation was rather stilted. Dick had to watch his language and his jokes. Her children weren't actually supposed to call him Uncle Dick, either, as the little twerps couldn't say it without smirking. Dick had remembered to send them a pound token for Woolworths every birthday and Christmas, and liked to think of them choosing racing cars or magic sets, but his sister had hinted that book tokens were more suitable. Anne was sweet, but she did tend to go on a bit about her children, their schools, their medical conditions and their certificates. Strange, really, when you looked at them. The boy, Jonny, definitely seemed odd.

The thought of food had awakened his senses to the smells from the new Indian takeaway shop below his flat. You had to hand it to those coloured gentlemen (as Anne would say) – they knew how to cook! He would often pick up a chicken tikka masala himself at the end of a long shift. And some onion bahjis. And the chapattis, and so forth. Actually, his neighbours, Mr. Ali and his soft-featured wife, were more respectful of the police than anyone else he could think of.

His thoughts turned again to his stomach and he tried to remember the contents of his own fridge. A couple of cans of

SKOL, milk (he hoped), and in the freezer compartment some of those crinkle-cut chips and a few faggots. And peas. He was sure he hadn't eaten those, and they might help him get into shape. It was as he hauled himself up from the settee that Dick remembered some post that he had stuffed into his jacket pocket that morning. One of the envelopes didn't look like a bill – that might be worth opening.

It wasn't a bill – it was an invitation on stiff card:

Special Private View
The Kirrin Island Experience
You are invited to an all-inclusive preview
Family only
RSVP Kirrin Enterprises

Well that was a turn-up for the books – Julian had remembered him after all. Good old Ju! Dick knew he'd see him right in the end! There was a letter and some roneo-ed details with the card – arrangements all paid for, staying at the pub in the village, interesting proposition etc. The directions showed a handy McDonald's on the way. He checked his shifts in his head. Oh dear, he'd have to wangle something, if that was the word. A few days off sick? He blushed at the thought, but he could feel that ankle twinge, definitely, and this was too interesting to miss. In fact, it called for a celebration. Time to pop downstairs for a takeaway chicken korma.

3

Julian Sends Some Invitations

It was unusual for Julian Kirrin to experience self-doubt. Indeed, as he tapped his cigarette into the heavy Habitat ashtray on his desk, and looked out of the panoramic window, his demeanour did not seem to admit of the possibility. Nor had it ever. Julian was a born leader; tall, straight and smart.

As a boy, he had looked at home in a suit. From Oxford to the Stock Exchange was a natural progression, as was promotion for such a personable chap. Julian was the kind of man whom people trusted, whom people believed. These were the qualities which helped a man go far in the city, and Julian had.

Julian's universe did not encompass failure. Divorce, when it came, was not a failure, but an option, a choice. He had made sure his wife had not suffered – financially, at least. This was 1979, and he liked to think he was a decent man. He pulled out the shiny end ball of his Newton's Cradle and let it swing back. The regular click, click, click encouraged his thoughts.

Of his son, certainly nobody could ask more. Hugh was the image of his father in mind and manners. He had followed Julian as Head Boy at his old school, excelling academically and charming all who met him. His recent graduation from Cambridge with a First in Natural Sciences had set him up for a glittering future. Certainly, the boy had shown a very keen interest in the Kirrin Castle project, forming a surprisingly close relationship with his cantankerous uncle Quentin. Exactly what the old scientist had done in those rocky underground rooms and tunnels was a mystery to Julian, but the one thing he did know was that it had never made him any money. Hugh knew what needed to be known, and that was good enough for Julian. He wasn't a details man.

"Get in on the ground floor, that's the thing to do," he had told his son earlier as they sipped coffee on the balcony. The potted rubber plant beside them reminded Julian of a David Hockney interior, which made him feel cosmopolitan. "Get in ahead of the market, Hugh. That's what makes the real money."

Hugh had listened attentively and learned. He had good reason to listen to his father. Their balcony wasn't on the ground floor – Cromwell Tower in the Barbican didn't have a ground floor. The flats on the twenty-fourth level had much better views out over the plaza, over the aspiring intelligentsia going in and out of the glass doors to their subsidised culture.

"That's what this project is – the ground floor. The middle classes are going to get tired of being herded into Freddie Laker's Skytrains or sharing with all those workers from Dagenham going to Benidorm to get plastered for two weeks. They want somewhere comfortable, with their own kind, where they can be looked after. And they won't mind paying for it."

"Absolutely Father, and we've got what it takes," Hugh had said enthusiastically. "But if we're going to be ready for the family I'd better load the Jag and get going. I've got a few things to take care of today before everyone starts arriving tomorrow. I only hope the trains run on time. You know what British Rail is like."

"Mrs. Thatcher knows, and that's good enough for me. Now

21

we have her in charge things will run on time. If she and Bianca ran the country they'd sort it out like a dose of salts. Bianca will have the schedule under control. She and I will follow down tomorrow in the Merc."

"You bet! She's always on top of things," Hugh agreed, as his father called her over from the large glass desk where she was sitting.

"One moment, Mr. Julian," she called from behind her typewriter. The golf ball bobbed and chattered, and she pulled the sheets from the roller, separating the copies from the carbon paper. She made her way towards them in her immaculate business suit and high heels. Bianca, Julian thought, could be one of those pneumatically perfect women who adorned shiny new cars in a magazine. So groomed, so capable, and refreshingly exotic. He twiddled his cuff links.

"Here we are, Mr. Julian. Your copy of the schedule for tomorrow, and one for you, Mr. Hugh." Her voice, with its delicious Latin accent, reminded Julian of Sophia Loren. She handed a piece of paper to each of the men. "The Kirrin Arms is booked exclusively. You and I will drive down tomorrow morning. Mr. Hugh will be there to meet and greet the family, and check them into their rooms. Mrs. Anne with two children and Mr. Richard with no children are to arrive at 11am at The Kirrin Arms in their own cars. Mr. Hugh will then collect Miss Georgina plus one, plus a dog, from the station meeting the 12.08 from Waterloo. Her ticket was delivered by courier on Wednesday. Mr. Hugh will deliver everyone to the island at 1pm for the picnic. Wine is organised. Mr. Quentin plus one will also be travelling by train. I will collect them from the station, and bring them over to the island at 3pm. Your introduction to the Castle Great Hall is timed for 3.30pm, and then guests will return to The Kirrin Arms for the evening. The Smugglers' Bar is booked for supper at 8pm."

"What a find she was," thought Julian. "What a change she has made to my life." Since Bianca had arrived everything had run smoothly, with all the annoying little details ironed out in advance. Some women had an instinct for these things, and he had been right to make her company secretary of Kirrin Enterprises. Some of his friends had called him a fool to let a woman have such control, but Julian knew a good thing when he saw it – brains and beauty in one package. Bianca knew things the investors didn't, and he trusted her completely. Julian had plans for her.

"Thanks, Bianca," acknowledged Hugh, casting his eye over the schedule. "You can leave a message for me at The Kirrin Arms if anything changes. The Ansaphone is installed now, or use the Telex. See you tomorrow."

Hugh waved cheerfully as he set off down the corridor towards the front door, picking up his bag and a briefcase as he went. Julian was confident about Hugh. He was a chip off the old block – someone you could rely on. The boy had coped well with the divorce, and he would cope with his plans about Bianca too, when he was in a position to announce them.

He watched her bottom under the tight skirt as she walked back to her desk. Was that a panty line? Or even the bumps from suspenders? As she sat down again and took the next folder, he had a good view of her legs. When this was over he would take her away for the weekend. Paris should do it.

With an exercise of will he turned his thoughts back to his business plans for Kirrin Enterprises. He took a long drag on his Lambert & Butler. SMOKING CAN DAMAGE YOUR HEALTH it said on the shiny silver packet. What rot! Julian was the epitome of self-confidence, and that was why he found it difficult to recognise the slight feeling of something awry that lurked at the back of his mind.

The acquisition of the Kirrin Island option from Quentin had been a coup – an opportunity too good to miss. Anyone who was not a complete fool made bags of money in the 70's, despite the difficulties, and Julian was not a complete fool. His irascible uncle, however, was always short of money, always working on schemes which came to nothing. Throughout Julian's life Quentin had been on the brink of developing a 'great gift to mankind'. That was what he had always called it, when they were children. Sometimes the government had helped, and sometimes foreigners with Astrakhan coats and interesting accents had provided funds, until Quentin had fallen out with them and there had been raised voices behind the doors of his study. Julian supposed the old man must have been on the verge of his great discovery at some point, and he had certainly commanded respect in the scientific world, but nothing had ever come of it. No Nobel prizes had followed, and certainly no glittering ones.

Nevertheless, it had still been a shock when Quentin's seemingly ever-tolerant wife Fanny had finally had enough and divorced him. There had been a marked change after he had been to that conference in South Korea. Quentin had been to conferences all over the world, of course, but this time he had come back a different man. Still irascible but no longer quite so unworldly, so distracted from reality. His new Korean backers had required him to move his work to their country for a year, and he had spent less time in his laboratories, and less still at home. Julian didn't know what it was that finally provoked Fanny into that bonfire of her husband's old plans and blueprints in the back garden, but it had probably been a long time coming. Quentin had done the decent thing letting her keep the cottage, but hanging on to Kirrin Island for himself was a bad business move for someone with no capital.

Julian took another pull on his cigarette. So – here he was, having already bought the freehold of The Kirrin Arms, along with several cottages as an investment, and made considerable changes to the style and clientele of the place. So far, so good. But that was the village – the mainland. The real focus now was Kirrin Island. The remains of the old castle on the island had really looked like collapsing, and when the normally supine local planners threatened him with a Compulsory Purchase Order Quentin had not been in any position to repair it, and the National Trust hadn't been interested. Julian had stepped in. He had been able to purchase an option on the island without having to make too many legally binding promises or spending too much of his own money. That's what he paid his lawyers for. He might be a bit stretched now, quite a bit stretched, but that was temporary. Phase One – the refurbishment of The Kirrin Arms and the work to make the castle sound and the tunnels safe – had been a lot more costly than he had planned. But risk was what it was all about.

That was what made the next few days so important. With a bit more investment the island would more than pay its way as an upmarket holiday venue. The middle classes were clamouring for an 'experience' with a bit of education and the nostalgia laid on thick, and the heritage market was set to boom.

Phase Two was where the money would really start to roll in. The Kirrin Island Experience would pull in thousands of visitors. Pitched right, it hit a prosperous demographic and the profile was bang on. The parents would come for themselves, increasingly affluent and too smart for Alton Towers, but after more thrills than the National Trust had to offer. Think what Beatrix Potter had done for the Lake District. And Kirrin Enterprises could offer more than a few dressed-up bunnies. He had the real thing. Or so he hoped.

The real thing. Julian had to admit that after twenty-five years the various components of the real thing were an unknown quantity. Time had not changed him, he felt. But the others?

Anne, dear Anne, would be enthusiastic. He had at least seen her in recent years and she would not be a problem, although that husband of hers was a bore. Julian had put a little work his way, though nothing important, and outside his office Rupert was even worse. Luckily, he was rarely around, leaving Anne playing around at counselling the prosperously troubled of Wimbledon.

Julian's thoughts passed on. Dick. Poor old Dick. Poorer, certainly, and younger than Julian, although he didn't look it. Julian felt mildly sorry for his brother – he was a decent type. But Dick was a nobody, a plod in the Met with a burgeoning waistline, and a poky little flat. Life had not been kind to Dick. Nobody had, except Julian. He remembered those discreet financial tips made, for safety, from public phone boxes. Real opportunities. But Dick never moved quickly enough; never wanted to be bold. Inside information never stayed that way for long and Dick was too slow. He'd be easy enough to persuade as far as the new plans went because he could do with a leg up financially. He might hanker after the chance to relive a bit of glory, too. Julian smiled at the thought.

So far, so good. His younger brother and sister would almost certainly stand by him. But there, thought Julian, old loyalties probably ended.

Because, of course, there was his cousin Georgina – George – fierce, and quite possibly almost immune to Mammon. The letter she had sent to Julian when he bought the island was bad, but nothing to the one Quentin had received when the news of his impending divorce and the division of the Kirrin properties had reached her. George had always believed that the island was hers, but Fanny had never done anything about it, and making the deeds over to Quentin in return for Kirrin Cottage had seemed the right thing for her to do when nobody visited any more. Julian had tried to pour oil on troubled waters with donations to the Women's Refuge, or Women's Freedom Group, or whatever grubby cause George was banging on about. It had seemed worth trying. But Julian's and George's paths had diverged so widely he couldn't predict whether she would be sensible and pragmatic, or whether she was still that fierce, feral child with whom they used spend their holidays.

There was a real risk that she would not come on board. Four out of five was what he needed. The fifth, Timmy the dog, was a problem, obviously. They were still working on the best approach and Bianca had been auditioning mongrels from agencies. Personally, he was against a stuffed version. George was essential to complete the group, and, Julian thought, to attract the slightly alternative demographic, the artists and rebels – so long as they had money and behaved themselves.

The Newton's Cradle had stopped.

"Well," he thought, going to the wall mirror, and minutely adjusting his tie, "everything will work out. This is a Julian Kirrin Enterprise." He pressed his finger to his outer eye, which was twitching again.

4

George is Rather Angry

For George, the prospect of a stretch in the all-female society of Holloway Prison would have carried less dread than the prospect of incarceration with her cousins for a weekend.

As a girl, Georgina Kirrin had always wanted to be a boy. As a woman of forty, she had little desire for their company. Specifically, her cousins Julian and Dick filled her with particular aversion. They were, to her, the epitome of two ends of the male spectrum: the overachieving and the underachieving. Anne was a spineless victim of gender stereotyping and male domination and there was no hope whatsoever for her. A pity, but there it was.

George stopped pacing her flat. It hadn't always been like that. There had been a time when she had grown to admire and envy her cousins with their unshakeable self-confidence and their air of being right at all times. They had made her happy.

The door to her balcony was stuck again, and it was hot, so she opened a window, leaning her head and shoulders out as far as she could. The view was not inspiring. The name of the Broadwater Farm Estate belied its concrete walkways and grey facades. She didn't usually give it much thought – too busy with her job at the Community Centre – but today she found some very different landscapes pushing their way into her head.

Beautiful ones, which didn't stink. Her cousins were part of it, inseparable from the memories. She wondered whether she should have read the smartly enveloped letter which was so obviously from Julian, and had landed through her letterbox like an Old School Tie at a jumble sale. Instead she had thrown it at the bin with a force which shocked even herself.

The thought of Julian reminded George, perversely, of better times. With a surge of feeling she remembered the island, always lurking somewhere inside her, though rarely allowed to surface. Her island. She had, eventually, shared it with her cousins, and they had enjoyed some extraordinary times there. Her best times. She had put up with the ridiculous school her father had sent her to, although she now regretted not rebelling properly while she was there. As a young adult, she had returned to Kirrin to visit her mother. Or was it really to visit her island? It hadn't been to see her father, at any rate, because he was rarely there, and if he was, he locked himself away in his study or the tunnels of Kirrin Island. Fifteen years ago, she had shocked everyone with the appearance of a son, Radclyffe, whose coffee-coloured skin had caused some raised eyebrows in the village when she had brought him along one summer, all bound up in a foreign-looking cloth sling, with no father, never mind a husband, poor little kiddie. The gossip had been the thrill of the locals for weeks.

George withdrew her head and flipped through the shelf of records before selecting one, pulling the little ball of fluff off the needle before lowering it onto the smooth outermost ring of the vinyl. It jarred a little before the crystal sounds of the acoustic guitar began. She perched on the edge of a shabby orange armchair where her dog, Gary, occupied most of the seat. The lurcher part of him was sprawling, and the bulldog part snoring intermittently. She drew out a tin and crumbled a fingerful of dried leaves, flattening them into the rolling paper, soothed by the ritual.

She had given her mother fierce but occasional protection during the final years of her marriage and now that was ruined, too. Outraged, George had stormed around in disbelief as her mother had settled Kirrin Island, *her* island, on her father. The almighty row that had blown up between George and her mother had caused a rift, and she had not visited for years. When news came that her father was handing the place to her eldest cousin her fragile relationships with the rest of her family had finally cracked. In place of dreams of her island she had channelled her considerable energy into causes which really mattered to people who needed it (and would wipe the smile off the faces of the financially superior). Even Julian's blood money, a rather substantial sum to her Reclaim the Streets Project, did nothing to heal the wound.

George licked the glue strip and sealed her roll-up. Flicking a lighter she lit up and took a deep draw. She and Julian had not seen much of each other since they had all left their snotty boarding schools. His career in the city and hers in the slums had diverged. He represented the Anti-Christ in a suit for most of her friends and she couldn't remember when they had last spoken. She had his last change of address card somewhere and a few years before, when she was marching through the West End reclaiming the night, she had thought she recognised a man in a pinstriped suit. But it had been dark, and to him she would have appeared only as another unkempt eco-warrior in unflattering clothes. They all had their uniforms.

Anne had tried. She had set up a ridiculous lunch party at her house some years ago, when Dick had sold his soul to the Commissioner of the London Metropolitan Police. Anne was a good soul, and George had felt enough curiosity to turn up, but the prissy front gardens and Anne's swagged curtains had put her off before she got through the front door. George *had* made an effort, though. A real effort. Gone inside with as best a smile as she could. Admired the fancy lunch Anne had laid out with such care. But it was all no good. After ten minutes of Anne's insufferable *niceness* and Dick's ridiculous idea that he was serving the people of the metropolis, she had left before she could do any real damage. She knew that Anne had been fighting back the tears, and she was actually quite sorry about that, but what else could she have done? She had had the secret Radclyffe growing inside her and she wasn't up to social niceties with anyone. And that was fifteen years ago.

Her roll-up was finished. She got up and threw it out of the window looking down into the gloom of the dusk, past the walkways, into the well of the estate. At least the rubbish that had accumulated over months had gone; the workers had been right to strike but it had been putrid and rat-infested. The 2CV was still there, stranded after its MOT failure, a bright green beacon with its striped roof, strangely un-vandalised. Perhaps it was preserved by a protective aura emanating from the stickers – the smiling sun of *Nuclear Power? No Thanks.* Did it fail to represent the kind of achievement that provoked vandalism, she wondered? She often asked herself why the people she lived among didn't rise up. She did her best to encourage them, standing at the bottom of the stairs with Socialist Worker, but she could hardly give it away. Friends told her sales were better in Hampstead. Her Women's Groups were a bit more successful but they only raised the consciousness of a small number, most of which had already rejected their middle-class backgrounds. Like George.

She was jolted back to the music – the one about paving Paradise. The record was old, and always stuck on the parking lot, repeating the two words over and over, like a jerky v-sign. She nudged the arm over the scratch. Her common past with her cousins was a long time ago, and the divergence so complete that her rejection of Julian's smart envelope was as automatic as a startle reflex. She might have remained at liberty longer if Radclyffe had not found it.

5

Radclyffe Comes Home

Radclyffe slipped in quietly through the front door, casting a glance back down the grubby walkway before clicking it closed behind him. He had learned to come in quietly. If his mother was asleep it was better to leave it that way, if she was running a Wimmin's Group it was worse. With his trousers ripped, zipped and chained, and his *Sham 69* T-shirt visible through the holes in his ragged sweater, he might have fitted in with the fashion sense of some of his mother's friends, but he was irrevocably cursed with the wrong chromosome.

He had learned to fend for himself. Like his gender at home, or so it sometimes seemed to him, his skin on the street didn't fit either – he was neither white nor black. He was a loner, though one who had found a few places where he had a role. School wasn't one of them, not often anyway, and nobody seemed too bothered about that. Career Opportunities didn't abound, or not the ones that school might suggest. He roamed the streets, walkways, and dark corners of the estate. Radclyffe, however, had learned that the walkways were as good as supermarket aisles for some products, and that this offered opportunities. He had started by selling pirated cassettes recordings, carefully made at home from records bought for the purpose, and had found a reasonable trade. This had built up quite nicely, and the new one from Boomtown Rats would bring in a decent return (he didn't like Mondays much himself, either). Recently, he had slipped into carrying and selling a bit of weed. Really just a very little bit; after all his mother had recently started smoking it. He was doing well, he was bright, he was careful and he was fast. He wanted things.

But first the kitchen. He set his ghetto blaster on the table, and was hewing the irregular brown loaf made by one of the Wimmin with the same fierce attitude to bread that she had to everything else, when he saw the envelope, crumpled on the floor where it had missed the bin. It looked out of place, gleaming cream, not brown, and with his mother's name and address in black fountain pen. Intrigued, he bent and picked it up, and pulled out the thick card invitation.

"Hey, Ma!" he called, able, like any streetwise fifteen-year-old boy, to distinguish real quality from the regular junk mail. He put his head round the door of the living room. "What's this?"

"What's what?" His mother looked up from a back copy of Spare Rib to grimace at Radclyffe's cassette player, which was pouring out a list of reasons she should be cheerful. Where had he got the thing, anyway?

"This! It looks like some free holiday shit. We never go on holiday."

"It'll be a disgusting money-making scheme. They always are," she replied, an ambiguous feeling of discomfort and suppressed curiosity rising up in her. Radclyffe groaned. She never shut up about that stuff. What was the point of sitting around in a hole and never having any fun? He tried again.

"No, but who's Julian Kirrin? And what is Kirrin Island? That's us – Kirrin."

George had never felt it appropriate to confuse Radclyffe with the mythology of her early years, and had avoided all references to her cousins or her own childhood. As she rarely saw any of them this had not been difficult. In her view it deprived Radclyffe of nothing except the possibility of seduction by capitalism, conformism and consumerism. Nor did she want to be reminded of her former longing to be a boy. The very fact that she had produced a son astonished everyone who knew her. She had loved him as a baby, of course she had, but they had had little to say to each other as he grew, and she had long ago given up on asking where he went and what he did. However, she did not believe in lying. Perhaps, just perhaps, they could see eye to eye on something. That would be nice, for once.

"All right, come here," she said wearily, closing the magazine and accepting that the subject could not be avoided forever. "It's like this. Once upon a completely different time..."

In the end, the battle of wills between a determined teenager with adventure on his side and a strong-minded mother torn between shunning all she despised and once again seeing a place which had been so precious to her could have only one result. In the back of George's mind was the thought that introducing Radclyffe to his extended family might be the chance to show him just how awful they all were.

Once she had submitted, the mechanics remained an obstacle. Skipping the bypass demo was not that much hassle, but transport was more of a problem. Since the 2CV had failed its MOT so hopelessly George had refused to buy another car, and looked down rather nastily on drivers. However, the railway was crap. Jimmy Saville might say it was the Age of the Train, but it wasn't the friendly railway she remembered. Since her childhood Dr. Beeching's axe had left the nearest station twenty miles from Kirrin.

She screwed up her courage and picked up the phone. She worried as he dialled that he might answer, but to her relief it was Julian's Ansaphone; "Got your invite. OK. I will come, and Radclyffe too, but need two rooms and a lift from the station." And then another. "And don't forget we are vegetarian. And we've got a dog."

Gary only added to the transport problems. It wasn't that George was so attached to him that she couldn't bear to leave him behind – God knows he wasn't Timmy – it was just that nobody else would look after him and she didn't approve of kennels. Too much like boarding schools. Ageing mongrels with the temperament of Johnny Rotten are not the easiest dogs at the best of times, but Gary added incipient physical breakdown to a foul temper and breath. Indeed, to George he exhibited most of the failings which in her view characterised the male of any species: moodiness, belligerence, meat-eating, poor personal hygiene, emissions of foul air from both ends and the desire to hump anything that didn't move.

She struggled briefly with the ethics, and the mechanics, of putting him in a box. Faced with keeping him under control in a railway carriage for five hours, she overcame the moral objection.

6

Arriving at Kirrin

Anne's odyssey began when the Volvo Estate had been loaded with every actual and every possible necessity that might be required over three days away from Wimbledon. Mrs. Finniston had been given a long list of tasks to be performed during her absence – no.17: scrub all skirting boards, no.18: vacuum underlay before replacing (disinfected) carpets.

Anne settled herself behind the wheel, tidied her already neatly dressed hair in the mirror, and turned with a bright smile to her children.

"Darlings, we're off! To a real castle on the dear little island where Mummy had so many adventures. Only just think, Uncle Julian is making it all lovely. What a wonderful time we are going to have! Now, I need to do a bit of concentrating. Daddy told me the car was a bit of a monster for a lady to drive."

She pushed a cassette tape into the dashboard and turned the volume up. Julie and Jonny were too busy squabbling over the window winders to listen properly and were soon making exaggerated vomiting sounds at the trilling musical version of the six times table.

Oh dear, mused Anne, as she hauled the steering wheel round with some effort, Jonny really should listen. His reports haven't been *awfully* encouraging, and Common Entrance is less than two years away. She so hoped he might go to Julian's and Dick's old school (as a day boy, of course) but the place was getting terribly competitive lately, and Jonny was so very sensitive and *individual*. She accepted he was not likely to be Captain of Games or Head Boy. Julie was a bit of a problem, too, as Anne's old school, Gaylands, didn't take day girls.

She switched off the cassette reluctantly and handed her children the *I-Spy Book of Historical Buildings* with a bright suggestion that there might be some really interesting ones on the way.

"Jim'll fix it for you…" sang Jonny, "and you…and you…"

Anne arrived early. Her natural enthusiasm to see what had been done at Kirrin had led her to get quite brave with the accelerator after all – these super Volvos were so safe and the A303 was quite a fast road. Crumpled McDonald's cartons had been added to the mess in the car, and Julie and Jonny were still fighting over the plastic distraction goods as Anne parked perfectly tidily in front of The Kirrin Arms. She stepped out and looked across the bay to dear old Kirrin Island, and her heart swelled up inside her chest.

"Oh look!" she exclaimed. "Look, children! It's just as if it's waiting for us! And look at our castle!"

There it was – Kirrin Island – jagged, familiar, and just far enough out to be a real little place of its own. The island seemed smaller than she had remembered it, but even from the mainland Anne could see that the castle was transformed. No longer largely tumbled down, it had been rebuilt into a sturdy square with two complete towers. There would be no mess from those noisy jackdaws dropping down on them now! Her eyes shone, and Jonny followed her gaze.

"May the Force be with you."

Anne turned around to smile at her son and was surprised by two things she saw behind him. The first was a rather smart black BMW parked closer to the quay with two swarthy? no, that wasn't right, two coloured gentlemen, standing by it.

"Goodness," she thought, "they have them down here as well. And such a nice car too." But she quickly dismissed her own prejudices. "And why not, of course. Times have changed. We're not that silly now." The second was that they were talking to a nice young man who, immediately he saw her, rushed over and greeted the three of them.

"Hello, Aunt Anne. Hello, twins. How super to see you!" exclaimed Hugh, a little breathlessly. "Some summer visitors. Just giving them directions." He gestured back towards the BMW. "Now, let's get your things into The Kirrin Arms, where you will be lovely and comfortable. We'll settle you into your rooms and you can freshen up while I go and collect Aunt George from the station. And then it's off to Kirrin Island! I'm really looking forward to one of your picnics. Father says they are literally legendary."

The Kirrin Arms was looking very smart, having been newly whitewashed with a freshly painted sign depicting the bay and the island. Hugh helped them with their bags and booked them into their rooms. He is such a charming and helpful young man, thought Anne happily, as the children scuffled up the narrow windy stairs.

Dick, too, had put his foot down in the Capri, glad to give it a good run. He had been ahead of schedule until he had diverted into the McDonald's off the bypass. Now he screeched to a halt across the end of the quay at what he hoped was a stylish angle, ready for a photo-shoot in which he stood leaning on the bonnet while a young lady draped herself somewhere and looked on admiringly. Sadly, there were no ladies looking on admiringly on the quayside. A few fishermen looked up from sorting out their nets.

Like Anne, Dick had been surprised to pass the smart BMW being driven away from the village by two black men in shades. If that had been in London and he had been on duty he would have pulled it over, obviously, but he was off duty and perhaps they were, too. He supposed even criminals took holidays. Then Dick frowned at himself. His early detective work with his brother, sister and cousin, had brought him into contact with lots of different people; swarthy men (as they used to say), foreigners with strange accents, even gypsies. They had generally assumed them to be dodgy back then, but that hadn't always been the case. Not at all. Dick's mind wandered back – Ragamuffin Jo, he remembered fondly. She'd been really nice, once you got to know her.

He reached behind the seat for his bomber jacket which dislodged a trail of fast food debris and a rattling can as Hugh advanced towards him from the front porch of The Kirrin Arms, holding his right arm outstretched.

"Welcome, Uncle Dick! Jolly good to see you! Aunt Anne and her twins are already here and settling in. Now, if you just take your bag in they'll book you into your room, and we can be off."

"Okey-Dokey!" he said. "Jolly good to see you, too!" Gosh, he was sounding quite like his old self!

There they stood at the crumbling little railway station. George, Radclyffe, Gary (in a box) and their rucksacks. If Hugh had failed to pick them out it would have been understandable.

Brought up on tales of George the fearless girl he had little chance of recognising the woman in the big CND sweater and green legwarmers. Radclyffe in his *Sham 69* t-shirt and Doc Martens, looking streetwise, stood out. The dog box clinched it. Plus, there wasn't anyone else at the station.

Hugh looked carefully at the teenage boy. He seemed wary, like an animal out of its natural habitat. He could be any one of those tribes of punks, or new-wavers. Hugh came across them on the streets when he went to the less salubrious parts of London. His friends promoted their records and concerts and sold expensive rip offs of their ripped clothes. Radclyffe was just another of the angry young generation. Or was he? He looked again. Hugh wondered if he had seen him before.

George had no such doubts. She was taken aback by Hugh's resemblance to his father. His hair was defiantly short – barely over his collar. Even the blue pullover, which would have appeared archaic to anyone in her part of London, could have been Julian's.

"Aunt Georgina, er, George," he offered, remembering to correct himself.

"Oh well, at least he hasn't tried to kiss me," she thought, giving the proffered hand a rather unnerving stare. Hugh was never unnerved. Well, almost never.

"Let me help with that" he offered, reaching for the box containing Gary, but recoiling as the occupier snarled, and the box jumped towards him.

Gary travelled in the back next to George, Radclyffe having immediately leapt for the front passenger seat so that he could drool over the knobs and dials. Hugh gave him more than a few sidelong glances. There was something about the boy…

"Aunt Anne is here, with Julie and Jonny, and Uncle Dick has arrived too," Hugh explained. George, looking out of the window at the changed landscape, barely heard him. "We're all going to stay at The Kirrin Arms. We've been doing it up, so there are some great rooms for you all. I'll take you and Radclyffe to dump your bags. Then I'll ferry us all over in the launch. It shouldn't take a jiffy. The famous picnic is all loaded up ready, and Father's over there now." They passed the old railway station at Kirrin Junction, now home only to a model railway exhibition. The bay came into view, pale blue-grey and glittering, and George felt a lurch of longing as she stared over the waves to the little lump of rock that was Kirrin Island. It *should* take a jiffy. Much more than a jiffy. The difficulty of rowing through the rocks to the place had been half the pleasure; the privacy guarded so fiercely.

"At least he hasn't built a bloody bridge to it," she muttered, as Hugh stopped by the old fishermen's houses, some now quaint holiday cottages with pretty curtains.

Once Hugh had helped George and Radclyffe to get their bags into The Kirrin Arms and everyone had made slightly awkward greetings they were soon climbing aboard the Pride of Kirrin, a good-sized launch of shining navy and red fibreglass. Radclyffe was gazing at another set of dials. His mother was not impressed, and glared hard.

"I have been in boat before," she said, disdaining Hugh's proffered hand. "And in my day, we *rowed* across. That is, I did. None of the others knew the way. They couldn't do it without me." And now here were Julian and Hugh doing it all, with or without her.

But the jagged little island caused a gleam of something in her fierce blue eyes. It was possible, just possible, that Julian might have plans which would rescue the place. She felt a small stirring of hope.

*

With the picnic basket safely at her feet, Anne's enthusiasm swelled. How cleverly George used to negotiate the rocks in her little rowing boat! How marvellously Timmy had rescued the treasure map as it fluttered out to sea! She was jolted from her reverie by the sound of crackly music: 'The Seaside Special comin' down the line...'

"Oh, Jonny, sweetheart! Not the transistor radio. We don't need it here, with all those lamenting gulls and darling, tame rabbits and...lovely things..." she ended rather lamely. It was such a pity that Jonny so rarely spoke. And when he did, he was terribly *unusual*. A very inward sort of boy. Her attention was caught for a minute by a couple of rather odd-looking men hanging about at the other end of the quayside. One wore a knitted hat pulled low over his brow. Anne thought the other had thin, cruel looking lips. They looked a bit dirty and unkempt. Two lots of unusual people in Kirrin already! Oh, dear, what could they possibly be doing here? Hugh, however, gave her a reassuring smile, which she returned gratefully.

George moved right to the front of the boat, and sat crouched in the prow, with her dog trembling in his box beside her, her face looking forward towards the island and away from her cousins. Radclyffe and Dick stood round Hugh at the wheel.

"Wow! Holy shit!" yelled Radclyffe as Hugh pushed the throttle forward, and the launch rose in the water and accelerated away. He eyed the gleaming dials, the chrome and the radio aerials with interest.

Anne hoped Julie and Jonny hadn't heard Radclyffe's awful swear word. George hadn't seemed to notice, or she would have said something. But now they were off! The little island was getting nearer and nearer and Anne smiled again. Her children would love it; she knew they would. Such a pity that Rupert couldn't be here, but he had been most firm about it; some heavy audit, apparently. The office needed him. Just for a moment Anne felt a little neglected herself. Really Rupert hadn't been terribly interested in anything much lately. That was rather a relief really, but as a trained counsellor she knew that it wasn't quite *healthy*. Still, as Rupert so often said, she needed her sleep, and he might as well stay late in the office working jolly hard. The school fees had to be paid, and Rupert *had* funded her counselling course. She could always watch re-runs of The Galloping Gourmet and practise her vol-au-vents.

Hugh carefully weaved between the buoys that showed the channel between the jagged rocks and around the island to the new landing stage in the natural harbour.

"That was quite a tricky way to row," said Hugh politely, once the throb of the engine had died away. "You must have been terribly strong, Aunt George. Father has told me how determined you always were." George grunted, slightly mollified, as she got out of the boat. Things might not be completely horrible. She opened the box and released a subdued Gary, who staggered out, the unfamiliar motions of the sea and the unfamiliar motions of the train having combined to disorientate the usually robust beast. Seeing some freedom, he was soon tugging on his leash as they unloaded the picnic and started to climb to the top of the island. George felt her legs tremble a little, as the island air – salty and grassy – wrapped around her face and crept into her lungs. Looking up, they could see Julian standing and waving. Anne's heart leapt, and Dick's too.

"This will be just like old times," they both thought. Even George allowed herself that possibility before her personal reservations overcame her once again.

"Oh well. If it is as horrible as I think it will be I can always put arsenic in the water and murder the whole lot," she thought to herself, only half-jokingly.

Once she had been helped out onto the little jetty, Anne pulled from her pocket a small black and white photograph of herself and her cousins, with their dog, Timmy, taken on Kirrin Island nearly thirty years ago. They were so innocent, so bright eyed, so Famous! Julie peeped over her shoulder.

"Crikey, Mum. Look at that hair band!"

"*Everyone's a Fruit & Nut case…*"

With a pained look at the twins, Anne drew herself up bravely. She had packed her hair band and she intended to wear it.

"We are all going to have a wonderful time," she repeated, trying hard not to let a little quaver sound in her voice, "and this time there won't be any dreadful adventures to spoil it!"

7

A Picnic on the Island

At last everyone was here. Julian eyed them speculatively as they gathered for Anne's picnic on the hill. This had been the first piece of placatory planning by Julian. Anne had wanted a picnic, and when he had thought about it Julian had realised its potential as a piece of nostalgia to re-kindle old bonds. That should set him up to introduce them to the re-furbished castle. It wouldn't cost him anything, either.

Anne, busy laying rugs, was clearly brimming with excitement and anticipation. Good. Dick was sitting down wheezily with his eye on the hamper. Good. George was staring towards the castle with her jaw thrust out. Not so good. The door was firmly locked for now. Uncle Quentin was due within an hour. Possibly good, but too much depended on George. Julian's niggle returned to irk him.

Anne had loved preparing the picnic for everyone and her excitement at the idea had stayed with her. She beamed. It was glorious sitting out in the sun, high up on the hill, looking down on the whole island.

"Kirrin Island really is a proper island isn't it, children – one you can see all of at the same time."

Julie raised her eyebrows and Jonny stared.

"*España, por favor.*"

"Spanish! Clever boy, Jonny! But *you* know what I mean

about the island, don't you, Ju?" she persisted.

"Of course I do, Anne," said Julian. "We can see the beach, the new jetty and the old wreck altogether. It seems much smaller now we are all grown up, but we can still keep an eye out for smugglers and ne'er-do-wells!"

Anne giggled and gazed around. Kirrin Castle in the centre, the little stream running into the shore with the wall of treacherous rocks guarding its entrance, the natural harbour, the caves and rock pools, the gorse patches and brambles, and all around the blue sea. It was perfectly lovely, although the addition of a small Portakabin just up from the jetty was rather a shame.

"Isn't anyone going to open the hamper?" said Dick. "We've carried it all the way up here, and I'm absolutely starving. What have we got, Anne?"

"Well, I've lots of things you will all remember." Anne opened the lid. "So, sandwiches, of course, ham and tomato, egg and lettuce, and smoked salmon, as we didn't have any sardines or, er, tongue. Hard-boiled eggs too, with salt to sprinkle on, plums, fruitcake, and buns. And we've got ginger beer to drink, just like we used to."

Radclyffe, Julie and Jonny stared. Julie looked distinctly underwhelmed.

"No crisps?"

"No Pepsi?"

"A finger of fudge is just enough to give your kids a treat."

Anne looked helplessly at Julian and Dick.

"All looks great to me. Thanks, Anne!" Dick said, filling his plate with sandwiches. "Waste not, want not."

Anne tried George.

"I'm sure they'll find it's super. We didn't have crisps, and we loved it, didn't we?"

"I used to give mine to Timmy. You'll have to take the lettuce out of Gary's sandwiches – it chokes him. I tried to make him vegetarian but it didn't work. And he doesn't like plums." George was becoming a little more expansive. "Do you remember that Welsh girl? Gypsy, I think. She spat plum stones at us on Kirrin Beach, or damsons, or something. Kept turning up and making out she was rescuing us. She had a thing about Dick…after their fight." She looked across at her cousin. Dick was too busy with an escaping slice of tomato to notice.

Gary was raising his back leg rather close to the picnic rug. George pushed him away, and started the Rizla ritual with her pouch. Anne looked worried – she hoped it was *ordinary* tobacco, but even that was bad enough. She was saved from having to ask George to put it away as she mooched off across the hill, flicking a lighter and cupping her hand round her roll-up. Anne found Jonny's asthma medicine in her bag just in case, and waved it rather pointedly. She shifted round towards the rest of her family with a little sigh.

The picnic continued for a while, the twins picking fussily at the sandwiches and muttering about the lack of tomato sauce. Radclyffe didn't pick – he was astonished at all this stuff made specially, and packed up, and then handed out with paper napkins. Did people really do this? Plates with little patterns on, little salt and pepper sprinklers and glasses for the drinks? He didn't know anyone who did. He quite liked it. It had style, and he might as well enjoy a hamper load of free food.

Anne's optimism returned a little as she saw Jonny, Julie and Radclyffe looking towards Hugh who was chatting away. She was sure Hugh would encourage the younger ones with his jolly, straightforward ways.

"Hugh," she said brightly, "Your father tells me you've learned your way round the island. I know he has told you all about the happy times we had here as children. Later on, you might like to take them off exploring. I'll come, too, of course."

"Certainly, Aunt Anne," replied Hugh, politely. "But you leave the little monkeys to me, and have a rest. I'll see they have a jolly good time."

Anne beamed and looked around to congratulate Julian on his super boy, but he was still scribbling in his Filofax. She leaned over and squeezed Hugh's arm instead.

"You really are a darling, Hugh. I'll write a few notes for you first, though, just so everyone is safe and well. Now then, children, who would like another egg and lettuce sandwich? Oh goodness! They've all gone! Now Dick, you haven't eaten them all have you?" She looked reprovingly towards her brother, who shifted a little and looked sheepish. "Plums, then? Julie, you be a hostess and hand them round. Yes, Jonny, you must have one, too, only let me peel it first. You know how sensitive your tummy is."

There was a girlish squeal as Julie stumbled.

"Oh, good heavens! Julie darling, are you hurt?" Julie's face was a picture of disgust.

"Uuurgh! Mummy, it's horrible poo! Get it off my shoe! Get it off now! It's disgusting."

The plums were scattered across the grass.

"Oh no, we can't eat those now." Anne had sighted the rabbit droppings. Her sigh was much bigger this time, and her lips just a little bit wobbly as she tried to smile again.

"*Opal Fruits! Made to make your mouth water!*"

Julie stared – Jonny could be surprisingly astute at times.

Ten minutes later Gary, having eaten the dropped plums, was vomiting loudly by the nearest bush and Anne was busy with the towelettes again because Jonny had somehow poured the ginger beer all over himself. How on earth had they managed before disposable moist towelettes had been invented?

The discussion about where Hugh might take the children exploring did not go well. The cliffs were too high and windy, the caves too dark and slippery, the sandy cove full of midges and the sea lacking in shade from the solar rays. The old wreck was far too dangerous, obviously. In any event, Jonny had not looked at anything except his transistor radio for the past quarter of an hour. He was wandering about with it to his ear, turning this way and that and fiddling with the aerial. Then he brightened up. The tinny sounds of the Radio Caroline jingle only added to the disturbance in the island air.

In the end, Hugh left because he had to see about something important. Perhaps it was about collecting Uncle Quentin on the launch? Her uncle would be joining them at some point soon, which made Anne just a little anxious. Uncle Quentin was a darling, of course, apart from that very unpleasant business of divorcing poor Aunt Fanny, but he had such a loud voice he might frighten Jonny, and such a way of rubbing old George up the wrong way. Julian had said that he might be bringing a friend to help him, now he was getting on a bit, so perhaps it wouldn't be so bad.

She sprayed insect repellent around vaguely, and applied a second layer of suncream to all the exposed skin she could find on her children. She had offered it to Radclyffe as well, as George didn't seem to have remembered to bring any herself. He was quite *dark*, she thought, but perhaps he could still burn. He had stared at her, astonished, and declined. A small scampering movement caught her eye, and her heart lifted. Surely that was a flash of bobtail in the distance. A little bunny, scampering across the grass.

"Julie! Look!" Anne called, delighted. "Just like *Bright Eyes*!" but her words died in her mouth as a dark shadow emerged from the bushes.

"Crikey Moses!" shrieked Julie.

"*Curly-Wurly out-chews everything*," said Jonny.

"Holy shit, Gary!" shouted Radclyffe.

Anne felt a nauseous lurch in her stomach as Gary disappeared into the undergrowth with the mangled remains of the poor Kirrin Island rabbit – perhaps one of the last of his breed. He was a terribly chewy sort of dog. Julian made another note in his Filofax.

Everyone was having such an interesting time that they hadn't noticed the black clouds rolling in from the sea. An ominous growl of thunder sounded. How many times had this happened before!

"Oh, goodness!" exclaimed Anne, as the big heavy raindrops started plopping onto the plates. "Do be quick, children! Where are your anoraks? Jonny, keep your asthma drops handy. Julie, do help me with the last few bits and pieces!"

Suddenly everyone was bustling about, packing up and bumping into each other. The rain was soon pelting down furiously, and the thunder starting to rumble out at sea. Dick looked in his sports bag, pulling out wine gums, sweaters and half-finished packets of biscuits – nothing waterproof – before grabbing the cake tin, upturning it over his head, and setting off at a lolloping trot. Julian put up his capacious golf umbrella, took the wicker wine basket (his contribution to the feast) and sauntered off towards the small Portakabin. Anne admired his easy grace under pressure, and how he was always prepared.

"Oh, do come along, children, we're getting soaked!" She

jumbled the remnants of the picnic into her big bag and, following Julian's lead, shooed them towards the Portakabin by the jetty.

George looked around for Radclyffe. Where was that boy? He was very good at disappearing when you were looking for him. Mooching around with the dog, probably. She felt the damp coming through the shoulders of her jumper. Oh well, she decided, he can find his own way back. Very soon the last of the bedraggled picnickers had disappeared inside the Portakabin and the square of grass where the picnic blanket had been was as wet as the rest of Kirrin Island.

8

Radclyffe Finds the Tunnels

Radclyffe was in the mood for adventure. He had followed Gary into a clump of bushes which made some sort of shelter by the cliff edge, where Gary settled down with his fresh meal.

Standing at the edge of the cliffs, he peered over at the powerful dark waters slapping the rocks, and a thrill shivered through him. He had scaled walls, plenty of them – graffiti-coloured and smooth – but this was something else. He was wet already, so he might as well give up on shelter and have a bit of fun. He grinned and, without fear, began to clamber down from the top of the cliff. The rocks were slippery, but Radclyffe had climbed worse things than this, and there were plenty of lumps and bumps to catch hold of. Just a few yards down, he was pleased to find a good-sized ledge, almost completely hidden from the top, which made a safe-ish place to plant his feet and give his arms a rest.

He stretched his fingers, one hand at a time, and looked out over the sea, his eyes half closed against the rain. It was pretty spectacular. Really noisy and powerful, crashing and sucking and crashing again. Radclyffe had never actually seen the sea before, or not since he was old enough to remember, and it was more impressive – much more – than the smelly and sluggish River Thames. The rain came harder. A mob of angry clouds was scudding in towards the island, and he thought about climbing back up. No – he was enjoying this. Carefully, he lowered himself until he was sitting on the ledge, legs hanging down towards the booming water below. He lifted one foot and circled his ankle. It felt good. Dangerous.

He sat for a minute, then shifted his weight and shuffled back, his bones uncomfortable. He leant back onto his elbow, stretched out behind him, but felt no rocky resistance and realised there was a space, grassy and dripping, but soft against his arm. Twisting carefully round he saw that it was a sort of opening in the rock, about two feet wide, or a little more, the edges cushioned by clumps of grassy mud. Perhaps the entrance to some kind of cave where he could shelter? His mother had gone on about caves the other day and Radclyffe had shrugged, but up here, facing the stinging rain and the thrill of a risky fall, he felt a kick of curiosity.

He shuffled round. If she had done it as a kid, he certainly could. Soon he had his head and shoulders through the space and could just about see what looked like metal rungs in the rocks leading down into the dark. It was practically a ladder. Practically *asking* for it. Slim-hipped and narrow-shouldered, he managed to wriggle through, and was soon feeling his way carefully down the metal bars, finding it easier than he had thought. After the storm outside it was quiet and still. A bit of light, filtered by scrubby greenery, reached through the opening.

Next, Radclyffe thought, I will find some sort of secret door – isn't that what happens? Or a bloody great room full of crown jewels, or something. Yeah, right – should've brought my shoulder bag, obviously. But after a few steps down he stopped and grinned. Was this for real? He stretched his arm out. Yep! Yep, with knobs on! There, set back into the darkness, was some sort of metal hatchway. He was even more surprised to find that when he pushed at the edge the hatch swung open easily and quietly on oiled hinges. Peering into the darkness, his eyes soon adjusted and he could see that the space opened into a tunnel leading back into the cliff face. Weakly glowing wall lamps of some kind created little islands of light, rather like the walkways of his estate at night. Radclyffe did not hesitate for a second. He stepped down and into the tunnel, leaving the hatchway slightly open behind him.

"This is more like it," he thought. "This is more like an adventure."

The lights were just enough to show him his direction. The floors of the tunnel were rough, and he nearly tripped several times as he adjusted to the downward slope of the rocky passage. He could have done with a torch. Wasn't that the sort of thing you were supposed to have in your pockets? There wasn't really anywhere dark in London. After about fifteen careful paces the tunnel turned to the left, and began to wind about. After a while, he could see light coming from under a heavy arched doorway on his right, which lay just ajar. Radclyffe knew how to be quiet. A new-looking padlock, incongruous on the thick oak door with its rusted metal studs, hung open in the hasp.

"OK," he thought. "Nothing ventured, nothing gained. Or, as they say at Broadwater, get in there, mate."

He pressed his face against the smooth-rubbed area of wood and took a breath. It was a damp smell, infused with rust and something else. Cautiously, he leaned his weight on it and inched it open, curving his face round the thick edge. There, beyond it, was a room. It was little bigger than his bedroom at home, but with rocky walls lit by fluorescent strip lights in the stony ceiling. Two large tables stood in the centre, and a wire mesh sort of cage or box – about as big as a packing crate. How strange! Uncle Quentin had been quite a famous scientist in his time, of course. His mother had grudgingly told him a bit about his use of the island for some secret sort of science stuff, but this room had certainly seen recent use. A sports bag lay on the floor and a Filofax and a glass Pepsi Cola bottle sat among the steel containers.

Radclyffe took two paces into the room and sniffed the air deeply. Musty and interesting. Very interesting. He could do with a drink, though, and the sports bag looked promising. He started to move towards it, but before he had time to investigate further he stopped and listened intently. A faint sound, which echoed slightly along the tunnel, told him he was not alone. The noise was indistinct. He couldn't work out whether it came from the room, from wherever lay beyond it, or from the tunnel he had just scrambled along. Did it matter? This island belonged to his uncle, and he was there by invitation. There wasn't any breaking and entering.

But Radclyffe was used to hiding and used to running, and something told him he might not be a welcome visitor in this strange place. Time to split. He cast his eyes round – no good hiding places here. A further door lay slightly open on the opposite wall, but that might be a dead end. He would have to risk it and head back the way he had come. Radclyffe trod as lightly and quickly as he could as the passage twisted back round and began to slope upwards again.

His heart nearly skipped a beat when he realised that the unmistakable sound of footsteps was now echoing in the passage behind him. They were not the furtive, careful steps of a covert pursuer, but rang out confidently, and increasingly close. He was beginning to feel sure that his heartbeat must soon add to the noise when the gleam of the inadequate lights finally revealed the metal hatchway. He had left it slightly open, but now it was pulled across. He put his palms against it and pushed. Then he pulled. It wouldn't budge, either way. OK. So now he was trapped.

Radclyffe knew what would happen now; he would be confronted. That wasn't unusual, and he had got out of worse situations, but this was new territory. He knew kids who found themselves in the wrong place and saw too much and some of them came to sticky ends in London. Was a man with an Uzi about to come round the corner and terminate him? Gary would have been a useful companion now, but he was outside and tied up. Radclyffe dropped his hands from the hatch and tensed his neck.

No stranger's hands grabbed his collar from behind. Instead, a friendly voice made Radclyffe lower his shoulders and turn to face his pursuer.

"Good afternoon, cousin," said Hugh in his easy manner. "Are you keeping out of the rain too?" Hugh's powerful torch shone disconcertingly into Radclyffe's face.

"Er, yes."

"Doing a bit of exploring?"

"No. Just, um, staying dry. Just here, in this tunnel."

"Find anything?"

"Er, no, not really."

Radclyffe blinked hard in the beam. He had been interrogated before. Being less than wholly white skinned he had been stopped on 'sus' and searched more than once. He had worked out how to blank plods, knowing just how much cheek and lip you could get away with before you got stuck in the back of the van. He was good at it; they'd never found anything and, so far, they hadn't planted anything either. But being interrogated by Hugh was different. He was family, sort of. He was polite. There was nothing to react against.

Hugh, too, was finding the encounter stranger than his manner suggested. Radclyffe, so different from his other relatives, had been puzzling him since he had first climbed into the launch and eyed up the controls. If he was the sort of street smart youngster Hugh thought him to be, he might be useful. Useful to the project. Julian might not have the insight to see Radclyffe's possibilities, but Hugh flashed him a smile, white teeth gleaming in the semi-darkness.

"I bet this is a bit different from home," he suggested.

"Er, yes." Radclyffe had relaxed a little, but wasn't going to drop his guard completely.

"Remind me, where is it you live?"

"North London. Broadwater Farm Estate. Know it?"

"I do indeed. Some mean streets! Lots of activity there. Lots of opportunities." Radclyffe wondered where this was going – a posh white boy after a bit of weed? Radclyffe wasn't seriously into stuff like that – not really. He certainly hadn't brought any with him.

"Sometimes," he responded, still wary.

Hugh grinned again – he was warming to his cousin. He knew what Radclyffe had just seen, and he could have a pretty good guess at the sort of things Radclyffe got up to in London. The boy has his head screwed on, he thought. He isn't going to be fobbed off with fairy tales about secret government contracts or Uncle Quentin's experiments. Hugh was silent, pondering his next move. He decided.

"Cousin," he said, and his voice was hearty and warm, "we have bigger plans than anyone has dreamed of. There is a fantastic surprise coming up, and everyone will know about it soon. Believe me it will be thrilling. But there is still some work to be done, and you and I need to talk. Come with me. I've a proposition for you."

The two young men walked off back down the passage. They were to discover they had more in common than either had expected.

9

Uncle Quentin Arrives – with a New Friend

Inside the Portakabin the rain was dreadfully noisy. Anne wiped her children down rather ineffectually, Dick steamed gently, and George stood looking through the window to the jetty. No-one said anything much until gradually the rattling on the roof died away and through it the sound of a powerful motor grew. Julian tapped his watched. He smiled in a very satisfied way.

"Aha! Bang on time! Even a rainstorm doesn't come between Bianca and her schedules. Here she is with Uncle Quentin."

He gestured with his umbrella. The little crowd peered through the window and down towards the jetty, and Anne reached for Jonny's hand. The launch had been expertly steered in by a tall woman in a red business suit which showed off her dark good looks. Hugh, appearing out of nowhere with Radclyffe, got there before Julian. He helped secure the boat to the jetty while Gary stalked up and down, eyeing up the new arrivals.

Julian led his troupe down the path towards them, shaking out his umbrella and smoothing his hair as he went. A tall, rather stooped figure stepped gingerly from the boat, smoothly assisted by Hugh. He was accompanied by a small eastern-looking lady, easily thirty years younger than him. She staggered a little in her dainty heels as Gary fussed around her, then smiled rather sweetly round at everyone. Julian stepped across to take her arm.

Once on firm ground the old man shrugged Hugh's supporting arm away and strode forward, waving his stick threateningly. "Call that bloody dog off, George. I assume it's yours. Now let's see; all my delightful family gathered round."

Quentin's delightful family stood stock still, with mouths open. All but Hugh, who was shaking the old man's hand warmly. George's eyes blazed. Anne found her voice first.

"Oh, Uncle Quentin! Er…Julie, Jonny! Come and say hello to your great uncle. He can, um, tell you all about his wonderful inventions."

Jonny, after a pointed nudge from Anne, removed his finger from his nose.

"Real tough toys for real tough boys. Tonka!".

"What's the matter with him?" boomed the scientist. "Well, hello, children. As your mother knows perfectly well, I can't tell you anything as all my inventions are secret. What I do is very secret." He made one of his glowering faces, so like George, and gestured them away with his stick.

Julie stared at Bianca's stylish shoes and glossy lips. Why didn't her mother dress like that? Uncle Quentin slapped a hand around the rear end of the new helpful friend.

"Yu Na, you see before you my niece, Anne. She is one of life's innocents, so mind your manners."

Yu Na laughed prettily and gave Anne a wink. Anne's face pinked as she hustled Jonny to one side. She had at first taken Yu Na for Quentin's nurse, but it was dawning on her that this was the new friend Julian had mentioned. Anne had been anticipating another scientist or laboratory assistant, or perhaps a soothing helpmeet for her old uncle, with grey hair and sensible shoes, who could find his lost glasses and make sure he ate his lunch. Yu Na had some rather intellectual looking glasses, certainly. She was also rather handsome and had a knowing look in her eyes.

"Hello, um, Yu Na. How do you do?" faltered Anne. After a moment's silence, she added brightly "Come along, children. Say hello!" They didn't, and there was another silence.

George, her mouth set in a straight line, was inscrutable. Quentin, however, opened his and laughed loudly. He placed a proprietorial arm around his companion.

"Well, you lot, stop gaping. It's all perfectly legal – we're married. Found her in Korea. South Korea, obviously. My Lab Assistant. Well, not just the Lab now, eh?" He pulled Yu Na slightly off balance and gave her quite a determined kiss.

"Oh Quentin, you naughty man!" she said, quite demurely, once she had surfaced. Her accent was gentle, and she sounded rather fond.

The silence was longer this time. Only Hugh appeared unsurprised, and made a slightly oriental sort of half-bow to Yu Na. The lady gave him an amused and perhaps rather tolerant smile and returned the nod.

"Married! Er...gosh! Um, well, congratulations, Uncle... and, um, Yu Na..." said Anne at last, tailing off with an anxious little sound. Dick became aware that his mouth was hanging open, and shut it, hurriedly.

"Oh God, Father," snapped George, suddenly. She kicked out at Gary. "Exploitative male bastard," she muttered under her breath. Gary looked resentful. Dick trembled a little in his Wranglers.

"Ah yes," exclaimed Quentin, looking up again. "You must be Dick. The greedy one. Bigger and fatter than you were last time I saw you. Where's your woman?"

"Er, hello, Uncle Quentin," said Dick. He stifled a sigh. "I'm still single, actually."

"Not a pansy, are you? Must be a bit of tail in tow somewhere, eh!" Quentin was roaring and came quite close to poking Dick in the chest with his stick. Dick squirmed. What did his decrepit old uncle have that he didn't?

Julian cleared his throat and raised his voice with practiced heartiness.

"Now that we are all here, let's not hang about. You can all catch up on old times this evening. Follow me to the Great Hall of Kirrin Castle!" He raised his furled umbrella to point the way and they all trooped up the hill behind him. Quentin kept pace reasonably well with Julian, and talked determinedly as they went.

"I know you city types are supposed to be clever, but I think all this holiday camp stuff is tosh. All my contacts in the States say that the clever money is in nuclear shelters. Every university over there has nuclear shelters in the basements."

"Come on Uncle, things aren't that bad," responded Julian. This was an annoying start.

"Not that bad! Wait till that idiot actor fellow Reagan becomes President. Everyone is afraid he'll press the button by mistake. Do you know his campaign slogan? *Let's make America great again!*"

"Oh dear, do you really think so?" asked Anne. She wished she had brought a more comprehensive first-aid kit.

"In America, they are planning for it. Nothing like that here, but one of my contacts sent me their plans. 'Protect & Survive' they call it. Tells you to lie in a ditch with a paper bag over your head! Pah! Now Kirrin Island would be just the job – deep tunnels, big doors, natural wells."

"Well thanks for the tip, but I think that a marketing plan based on the Apocalypse is too much of a challenge even for me. But, if it ever happens I promise you can all have places."

Several steps to the rear, Bianca and Hugh stopped. She brushed a speck from her skirt and took in the island at a glance. Hugh spoke quickly and quietly, under his breath. With a sideways look she replied in breathy accents.

"I see. Yes, I see it clearly. But you can leave your father to me and let me do my work. I still have more to do, and he wants me here to help with his presentation, I think." She winked, unsmiling and cool, tapping her shining briefcase.

"Later on, I'll introduce you to Radclyffe," Hugh smiled. "Perhaps not just yet, though." As they reached the castle he led her through a side door which avoided the Great Hall.

10

Inside the Great Hall

The Great Hall of Kirrin Castle looked splendid. Julian had bid on a good collection of would-be medieval artefacts from the liquidation of a failed theme hotel, one or two of them actually genuine. The suits of armour, as erect and straight backed as Julian himself, looked quite convincing from a distance but the shields were plastic, and the great table underneath the tapestry cloth was plywood. Viewing it all with fresh eyes, Julian was slightly concerned his budgetary restraints left it looking just a little like a suburban drama company's production of Camelot. This was not the plan in the longer term, of course – his ambitions were more Technicolor. He wondered whether Hammer horror films ever sold off their old sets and costumes?

Earlier that day, Julian had stood in front of the throne and in his mind's eye seen it filled with deep-pocketed merry revellers, all quaffing from tankards and served by maids and wenches in colourful costumes. Weekly banquets would turn a steady profit. Bianca had helped him with his research there, and he'd put on a couple of pounds. He'd had some artist's impressions done and looked forward to the first mini-banquet with his cousins. This would take place tomorrow evening and wouldn't be the full works, but a scaled down trial run of the main features, an attempt to seduce his relatives into playing ball with more splendid events in the future.

Julian had been pleased to find that the type of feast he intended to serve up was surprisingly cheap. Give the English a hunk of meat and, as long as it went alongside a 'historical experience' they thought they were getting good value. No prawns, fondues and cherry decorated gateaux would be required – the punters wouldn't miss the vegetables and fiddly bits that took so much labour to assemble. He had also calculated the saving to be made on washing-up staff and equipment by doing away with cutlery. He regretted that it would still be needed for breakfast, but you could hardly expect visitors to tackle a Hearty Yeoman's Full English Breakfast with their bare hands. And breakfasts there would be, once the rest of the castle was furnished as a hotel. He'd been unsure about the cleaning bills for the costumes, but Terylene tabards would take the worst of the mess. Mead would be carefully rationed, or perhaps a nice expensive extra.

But that wasn't enough. An old castle was an attraction, and an important one, but it wasn't unique. People would pay through the nose for a banquet, but this venture was something more – not just 'heritage' but 'character.' Julian's plans were more complicated and more exciting than those of his fellow entrepreneurs because there was something else – something really special. Julian knew that if he could offer the more recent history of adventure and treasure with the *real* people in it there would be a premium. What would eager visitors pay for public appearances by real famous people? *That* was unique. He needed the family firmly on board, with himself in charge of the oars, the tiller and the back-up motor. Would his relatives do the business once a month? More? What would he have to pay each of them? This weekend was crunch time.

Kirrin Castle had been a place of innocence, mystery and adventure, but it could never be that again. Entrepreneur though he was, Julian felt a twinge of regret. He had loved this island very much. Still did. It had to be *this* venture, or the possibility of the island being preserved in the antiseptic aspic of the National Trust. Choices had to be made, and you couldn't live in the past. Julian felt sure he had been right, and anyway there was no money in a nature reserve.

However, he could not have complete confidence that George would agree. She had always treated the castle and the island as her own, although the deeds had never been in her name. Even now, Julian had only an option on the island, which technically Quentin still owned. That would be sorted out PDQ, obviously.

"How absurd," he thought. "When we first came to Kirrin George wasn't even going to let us visit the island. I am going to share it with anyone who will pay." And they needed to pay. The structural repairs had cost shedloads more than he had anticipated. Julian had sunk all he could afford into Kirrin, and more. If he couldn't get his investors interested he would be sunk, no matter whether he gripped the oars or not. With Kirrin Enterprises so pushed, outside investment was needed and celebrity endorsement by his own family was the way to get it.

The newly studded door stood before him, and he held its great key in his hand. It was time to take the plunge.

Anne had begun to chatter excitedly and fidget around the twins as they all stopped just outside the castle.

"I can hardly wait! Julian is so clever, and I know it is going to be marvellous. What do you think, Dick? George? Is it bringing back memories? Is it making you…"

Julian turned with his back to the door, cleared his throat, and began his pitch.

"Here we are – together again and back at Kirrin Castle. We will shelter here just as we used to. Just as many have done before us. But this is no longer a Kirrin which is decaying and crumbling away – it is a Kirrin which has been saved, strengthened, restored and, dare I say it, improved." He could have done with a bit of Elgar. "As you step inside, remember that it has been rescued. Rescued in a way worthy of its history. Saved for posterity. In a way, saved for *you*, George. Welcome to Phase One of *The Kirrin Island Experience!*" He straightened his back and pushed open the door.

By unspoken consent, Anne and Dick moved aside, and George was the first to step through the archway, with her chin jutting and her hands curled tight in her pockets. Her eyes were actually screwed shut for a minute, as the others crowded in behind her. She breathed deeply, nostrils flaring at the smells of plaster and varnish, and opened her eyes. Sweeping the interior of the hall with a piercing and almost hungry look she took in the theatrical set, the gold sprayed plastic goblets, the fibreglass deer's heads mounted on the walls, the flaming torches whose bulbs lit up at a flick of Julian's fingers on the master switch, standing, as he quickly did, halfway down the room on a wooden dais. A dangerous silence cut the air as all eyes swivelled to the tight and trembling face. The voice, when it came, was very quiet.

"What is this…this *stuff*?"

"George," he said calmly, stepping down and moving towards her.

"Stop there. Don't *George* me. Restored, you told me. Restored." Still icily slow and low.

"George? I know it looks different, but it's safe. *Safe*, George.

My, er, *our* castle is safe. Saved." She advanced slowly towards him, her fierce glare fixed right into his eyes.

"I don't like it. It's ruined."

"George. George, you are understandably loyal to this marvellous place. I am too, George. You see it *was* ruined and I have saved it. You can't imagine how awful it had become. Just rubble, really. What would have happened to our castle without this preservation work? Who else was going to do anything to sort it out? No-one but me. I know you wish you could, but that's not possible. Who else could stop it crumbling away to nothing?" He really felt that way. However, he realised uncomfortably that George didn't.

"Why is all this awful stuff here? Can't you all see it? Anne? Dick? Can't you see the…" George stopped, with some effort and looked into the faces of her cousins, both so eager. "I'm going. Don't follow me. It's *my* island. You know it is, *morally*." She threw that last word back at Julian as she left the Great Hall, pushing past the bemused figure of Hugh and the resigned shrug of Radclyffe, who had both just appeared at the door, rather like sentries. Hugh turned back down the path to see where his aunt had gone.

There was an awkward silence. Jonny's head swivelled round to look at the door his aunt had just flounced out of. For the first time since leaving London, he smiled.

"*Ooooh, you are awful, but I like you…*"

Julian cleared his throat, the sound echoing around the hall. He pondered over the likely next move on George's part. George had always done this. She had been a furious child, and that hadn't changed, obviously, but Julian had always managed to talk a bit of sense into her. Entrepreneurs were always hopeful and Julian pulled his lips into a smooth smile. He would find her and soothe the trouble away; she had always come round in the end, and he, Julian, had generally been the one to do it. But his eyelid was still flickering, and George wasn't the only member of this family.

"Radclyffe!" he said, mustering all his considerable *sangfroid* in front of the others. He had been startled at this scruffy street urchin, so unlike his own son, and had decided he probably didn't have much value in terms of publicity. But maybe there was something he could do which the others couldn't.

"Ah, Radclyffe, my boy. There goes George. Good old George, full of spirit! I'm sure you know that your mother and I didn't always see eye to eye immediately, but we always agreed in the end. She'll come round in time. What do you think? Magnificent, isn't it?"

Radclyffe shrugged – he'd never seen anything like it except perhaps when his mother had dragged him round the Tower of London to show where rebels were martyred and executed. It was just about the only place she had ever taken him. Actually, no, it wasn't, he remembered. There had been the Natural History Museum, when he was about six or seven. There had been this enormous great fish. No, a whale. A huge blue whale. Ma had told him about how people hunted whales, killing them for greed, and he had gazed at it, stiller than he had ever been before. That was a good memory. Anne's voice piped up, echoing round the castle and jolting him back to the others.

"Oh dear, poor George. She seems a bit upset. I wonder if she would like to try a glass of Lucozade? It's terribly good if you need perking up." She beamed around. "But Julian, *I* think the castle is lovely! Isn't it children? Quite magical and *so* real. Just like stepping back in time. Look, there are swords and everything."

"Yes, good show, Julian," said Dick, looking at the armour and the clubs, and wondering what the SPG might do if they all had those. He liked the look of the huge table set for the banquet which was on Julian's schedule for tomorrow evening. Everything must have cost an awful lot of money.

"Well, I'm glad you like it, but of course this only Phase One – there's more to come yet. I'll tell you about that tomorrow. This is, shall we say, a sneak preview. Shame about old George, but we know her, don't we? She'll sulk a bit, but she'll come round. She always did. Anne, you might have a word with her later – er, girl to girl. And she can't get far, can she?"

His earlier niggle of doubt, though, had grown. His natural enthusiasm could only sustain him so far against the sudden storm of his cousin's reaction. They all stood in awkward silence, until it was broken by the sound of hurrying footsteps on the cobbles of the courtyard.

"Father!" shouted Hugh, coming in breathlessly through the big doors. "It's George. She ran down to the beach and started kicking stuff around, and I've just seen her pushing the old rowing boat down the beach. I didn't realise it was still there."

Suddenly the Great Hall was deserted as they all rushed out to stand on the hill and peer down onto the beach. There she was, George, Gary with her, rowing bravely away in the shabby little boat. She was a little unsteady at first, but soon the oars were working together as she pulled towards the old wreck and then circled round it, heading for the mainland, as she had so many times in the past.

11

George at The Kirrin Arms

George reached the little quayside at Kirrin Bay with both fear and satisfaction, and moored the boat up tightly. She was sopping wet and it had been a near thing. The old boat had leaked badly, and wouldn't be fit for a return journey without some serious patching up, but that could be done; most things could be patched up, if you knew the right way to go about it. Only I don't, she said to herself. And neither does Julian. We're rubbish at it all. She stood for a moment and gave her boat a rough pat.

"No-one has messed about with you, yet, though," she said gruffly.

She checked the mooring was secure, coaxed Gary out, and stood up very straight. Gary wobbled a bit, but then followed her as she made her way along the quayside to The Kirrin Arms. Dogs were allowed inside, but Gary was dripping wet and too good at picking fights to be trusted, so George towelled him down with her already sodden sweater and tied him up to a post without much regret. A dog bowl of water had been provided, and she left him to it.

She was feeling a bit better, and pushed her way into the pub and up the stairs to her room. She ran a bath, grudgingly appreciating the plentiful steaming hot water, which never worked properly in her flat. She dumped her dripping clothes in a heap on the floor, and climbed in. There was complimentary soap and shampoo, and even a little inflatable plastic pillow to rest her head on, with suction pads to keep it in place. The water looked greenish in the coloured bath, a bit like the sea in the Autumn.

She closed her eyes and thought back over the last half hour with some astonishment and more pleasure than she had felt at anything else for a long time, despite the frantic bailing out every couple of minutes, which she had had to do with cupped hands. It had all happened quite quickly. After Julian's revelation of the castle interior she had pounded at a furious pace down the path from the castle with tears and drizzle in her eyes. She had smudged them away with her fists and gritted her teeth. How had it all gone so wrong? Why hadn't she been around to keep her island safe? She had left it for too long.

At that moment, rushing away from them all, she had wished for just two things. The first was Timmy. Dear old Tim, who would have lolloped along beside her, and pushed his head soothingly into her hand. There wasn't anyone else who understood her the way Tim had. Not even close. Not Gary.

The second thing she had wished for was her old rowing boat. A strong bout of vigorous rowing had always helped to calm her when she was at her most troubled, and her boat had been her key to escape so often. Well she couldn't have that, either. It had probably been 'dealt with' by now. Taken for some decorative purpose for tourists to gape at, or just disposed of. That was when she had reached the little beach on her island, and kicked around in the piles of stinking seaweed in a tumble of misery, sending the flies up. And that was when she had found it, its flaking red-painted wood hidden under the rotting heaps, but miraculously still whole. Her heart had beaten faster as, searching under the tangled fronds, she had uncovered the oars and slipped her hand around the smooth, well-worn ends. Sometimes good things happened.

George soaped herself thoughtfully, looking at her sturdy body. It was not as strong and capable as it had been, certainly, and she had never bothered to take up jogging like half the world seemed to be doing, but her navigation through the rocks had been perfect, and she had enjoyed the fierce physical exercise. Her arms would be stiff later, but what did she care? Miraculously, Gary hadn't been sick, though he had cowered quite pathetically in the bottom of the old rowing boat. Not like Tim. Tim would have sat up excitedly and barked at the gulls and the waves. Still, here she was at Kirrin Quay, under her own steam, and ready to get away from her exasperating family for a while. She ducked her head under the water and rinsed the shampoo away, then climbed out onto the mat and sat for a minute on the side of the bath, rubbing her hair dry. What she really needed now was a good drink and the company of some genuine Kirrin people.

As a child George had not been allowed in The Kirrin Arms. Quite apart from the law, it had always been full of people you were told you wouldn't want to meet, or so her mother had always said; gypsies and smugglers, George had supposed at the time, or perhaps just ordinary people who didn't own farms and islands, and do scientific things in secrecy. They sounded to George just like the kind of people she had always seemed to get entangled with in the school holidays. True, Julian had ponced up the guest rooms, and there was a smart dining room theatrically called The Smuggler's Bar, where visitors from outside of the village were firmly directed, but he hadn't yet done up the public bar. This was doubtless on the agenda, but the locals were resisting and Julian was holding fire for now.

George pulled on some dry clothes. It was early evening now, and after all that stuff about her island she wanted some real working-class company; sons and daughters of the proletariat. She made her way downstairs and went outside to check on Gary, who was dozing noisily. He'd do where he was for a while yet. She remembered the working men and women who had peopled Kirrin during her childhood; they'd always seemed to find time away from their chores to spend hours talking to the children and telling them tales. Some of them might be still here.

The public bar at The Kirrin Arms was everything that modern brewery chains were trying to do away with; dark and smoky, with low ceilings and beams that were at the perfect height to bruise skulls. Collected from the shore a century ago, after a storm had wrecked some poor vessel, they carried the skin from the foreheads of unwary visitors, of which there were very few. Several heads turned as she walked in. A woman in a pub alone was considered suspicious, especially outside London, but that was too bad. She ordered the local ale, insisting the barman pour it into a pint pot after he delivered it, with a bit of a sneer, in a 'ladies' glass'.

"At last," she thought. "At last, I'll meet some genuine, honest ordinary people." She settled herself on a sticky barstool, took a good swig of beer, and had a look around. The old place was fairly full, considering it was still very early. Most of the tables had groups of people sitting around, and most of them were drinking beer and smoking. No-one had a Filofax; things were looking up. Now, could there be anyone here she recognised? Some of the people were youngsters, clustered around a juke box which wasn't working and whacking it with flattened hands, but on the whole the drinkers were from the older generation. Her attention was caught almost immediately as a face revealed itself through a particularly evil haze which surrounded the table next to the bar. She looked puzzled for a moment, racking her brains, then grinned in delight.

"Oh, goodness!" she gasped, uncharacteristically. "It can't be…" she looked more closely. "Yes, it is! Coastguard! Dear old Coastguard!"

The weather-beaten face, yellowed beard spilling onto a barrel shaped body, peered out of its dense surround and coughed messily.

"You what?"

George took several more gulps from her glass. This stuff was strong. Good. She smiled, her blue eyes lighting up now her eyebrows were not lowered.

"Oh, Coastie, I can't believe you're here. Right here in The Kirrin Arms! I remember you so well. We used to come and see you whenever we went for a walk along the cliffs. Years ago. You used to sing sea shanties in your shed as you whittled those marvellous toys for your grandsons!" What was happening to her? She was turning into Anne.

"You what?" He tapped his pipe and stared.

"You know – when we used to visit you during the hols." She spoke very slowly and loudly now.

"Eh?"

George moved closer to the old man and crouched at his chair. The others round the table looked on without smiling, mouths somewhat open.

"It's me, Coastie. George Kirrin…er, Georgina?"

"You what?"

"I said IT'S ME. GEORGE – Quentin and Fanny's daughter! From Kirrin Cottage."

"Alright, I'm not bloody deaf."

"No, of course not." George was flustered for a second. She finished her pint and sat a little tentatively on the chair beside him, leaning her chin on her hand, elbow propped on the damp bar. "Oh, Coastie, I'm having a bloody awful time. I hate some stuff at the moment. I live in London now and it's not very nice, actually. I do some good things, I think, but I wish it was the time when we used to row off to the island or walk along the cliffs and visit you on the way. DO talk to me. Please. I need it, I tell you." The old man looked at her, apparently without recognition, and she wriggled. "Well perhaps…er well, there is something I would love you to do. Could you perhaps sing one of your sea shanties? Just a bit? It would be…" what would it be? "…perfectly lovely." Had it taken only one pint to talk like this? She would be wearing a hairband next. The old coastguard sat up straight and jabbed a finger in her chest.

"Who do you think I am? Captain Birdseye? There's a Traditional Folk Night on Thursdays in The Smugglers if you want to pay."

George's face reddened. She felt a bit awkward – more than a bit.

"Bloody barmy!" he muttered. And taking a good long pull on his pipe he exhaled in George's direction, before returning to his pint.

George turned away to hide her disappointment. As a child, she had liked the coastguard very much, and George had not liked many people. He was old, though, and probably didn't remember.

Not usually one to avoid confrontation, she thought this time she would get another drink and move on. She had just spotted someone she definitely wanted to speak to. There she was, button-eyed with a huge smile above her jelly chins, sitting on the far table with a packet of pork scratchings and a sherry. She was the very picture of a cheerful old lady who had spent most of her adult life as cook to a fine and appreciative family like the Kirrins. Dear old Joan, or was it Joanne? Or even Joanna? None of them had ever been quite sure. Somehow her name seemed to change slightly between one summer hols and the next. Her wonderful cooking, though, had never changed. She had been a staunch defender of Timmy, and the rock who George's mother had leant on for years. They could not have managed without her. Indeed, rumour had it she had only stopped working for Fanny because she had won a couple of thousand on the football pools, a few years ago.

And Joan, at least for now, seemed happy to talk about the old days. She grinned up from her glass and laughed in recognition, false teeth slightly askew.

"You! Master George from Kirrin Cottage. Or Miss George, I should say. Or Mrs.? No. Not Mrs., I shouldn't think. Well now, this is a surprise. You haven't been down for years, though, have you? And your mother would love to see you once in a while. Love to. Well, come and settle yourself down next to me. There." George squeezed herself next to Joan and took another gulp of beer, thankfully. Joan continued. "You kiddies – ooh, I remember those meals you used to put away."

George felt more reassured. Joan had been practically part of the family for years. She had pretty well run the cottage, and was clearly still a local, despite her rather incongruous leopard skin handbag. There was a scarf, too, George noticed, decorated with snaffles and bridles and horses' heads. Presumably they had been bought with her winnings. George spoke quite brightly.

"Oh yes, Joan! We always loved everything you cooked for us. Do you remember what we used to say? Scrumplicious! Or was it delumptious? Those wonderful plum cakes, and home-cured hams. All those picnics! Do say you still make scones every tea time!" George stopped. She was halfway through her second pint and felt herself sounding more and more like her youngest cousin. She would have to get a grip.

"Oh yes!" enthused Joan, wobbling vigorously as she nodded. "I do. And chocolate brownies now. Betty Crocker Mix, it's called. You get a little cardboard baking tray thing to put the mixture in, so there's no dirty washing up. American, you know, but your mother never minded. Mind you, there was good cause to stay out of the way in the kitchen in the last few years. It wasn't very nice. Not very nice at all. There was all the tempers going on, and you'll know what I mean by that, I'm sure. And what with Mr. Kirrin's comings and goings, shall we say? Your poor mother had enough to put up with. It's no wonder she's turned er...gone a bit..." Joan's words were lost as she sipped her viscous scarlet drink. George felt downcast – so even dear old Joan was a victim of commercialisation. And her mother was fragile, certainly, having been through such an awful time. Guilt wasn't feeling very comfortable.

"You can't get 'em in the Village Shop, the cake stuff, I mean. It's full of them bent froggie bread rolls and stuff now, so I stock up in Tescos. So much cheaper. I use me bus pass and go into town."

"Well, we loved your tarts and pies, Joan," said George, uncomfortably aware of trying to drag the conversation back into that dubiously sunny past. "So did Timmy, I'm afraid."

"That Timmy, bless him! I remember him getting blamed for more than one stolen meat pie from my larder, but we all know who really stuffed his fat little face with it, don't we?"

"Do we? Oh Joan, no, surely not! Dick?" It had to be. His

appreciation of a good cake was still visible these days. "Well, darling Timmy ended his days many years ago." George bit her lip a little. "I wish he was here now, Joan, more than anything. I hope he didn't steal pies when I went away to college. Sussex Halls of Residence wouldn't let me take him." George thought wistfully of those student days of Political Studies and like-minded friends, even though she had dropped out pretty quickly.

"Oh, no, he weren't no trouble – not for long anyhow. It was the gamekeeper sorted him out, poor old thing. Shame. I liked old Tim."

"Sorted him out?" George felt a cold hand creeping round her heart. "No, Joan, you're forgetting. He was so terribly old by the time I left, poor Tim, and Mother told me how he fell off the cliff trying to chase a rabbit."

"Did she now?" Joan smiled. "Soft-hearted old thing."

"What do you mean? It was a terribly sad accident." The most bereft I've ever felt, she realised.

"Poor creature," Joan spoke quite gently. "He was *never* a bad dog – *never*. Just getting a bit confused, really. Like the rest of us. Once he started worrying the sheep, it was the kindest thing to do."

George choked, and stumbled for the door before anyone could see the tears in her eyes.

Joan's chins wobbled comfortably as she spoke to the coastguard.

"Go on, now, Fred – get me another sherry. No, make it a port and lemon – I'm feeling all of a do. Poor girl. Mind, it's about time that young lady started visiting her mother a bit more."

"Oh, aye, that reminds me, Joan. They're all back, y'know."

"Who's back?"

"The Kirrins. The other kids, as they were. Come yesterday,

they did. Stayed here, in the new rooms upstairs."

Joan swilled the rest of her glass down in one.

"All of them? I suppose it's something to do with all the changes going on; the island and all that. An adventurous lot, though a bit selfish in some ways, now I think about it. Not that Miss Anne so much – she was thoughtful enough, and helped me a bit. But I could tell you a few home truths about one of that little bunch – things what'd put you right off your beer. Yes, even you, Fred Pitts."

"Well go on, then." A wiry woman with a mop of black curls and a Welsh lilt to her voice was wiping down the tables. She paused and looked hard at Joan. "You can't stop there."

"Yes, what, Joan?" Everyone was interested now.

"Well, now, some of you knew them nearly as well as I did. Like you, Jo."

The wiry little woman grinned.

"Oh, yeah, I knew them. Used to spit damson stones at them, I did. Really wound them up. Had a bit of a punch-up, too. They needed me alright when it came to it, though. I don't reckon they'd be around now without me getting them out of a few dodgy places. Got themselves into the papers, they did, but not me. They were quite good times, though. Quite good. And I've often wondered about them. You know – what they're doing now, and all."

"Have you now? Well, they was all so full of them *pleases* and *thanks awfullys* and *I say, Joan, you're a marvel*, but what it comes down to is one of them, at least, was a piece of work."

"Go on – who was? I want to know, Joan."

Joan settled herself comfortably. "Like I say, I won't speak a word against Miss Anne, and George was an angry so-and-so, but straightforward enough, and honest as they come. I liked her well enough. Dick, now, he was just a bit of a greedy one – good natured and no harm in him. But that Julian, he was the odd one in my books. Very polite, very proper, but always gave you the feeling that he was a bit better than everyone else. A superior so-and-so. Nose up in the air – liked to be called *Master* Julian, giving orders left, right and centre. Caught him out once, I did, though. I don't *think* he was trying to do Marge out of her proper payment for torch batteries, though I wouldn't swear it on my mother's grave, God rest her soul. He said he'd given her five bob. She says it was two threepences, not two half-crowns. She was getting in a bit of a state, when I come in her shop, just behind, for some potted meat, I remember. I says, 'Now then, *Master* Julian, are you sure you're right?' He marched off with his nose up, but his face were three shades redder for that! *Might* have been an innocent mistake…*probably* was, if I'm honest…but I was never sure. Anyway – he didn't like being told."

A lean and handsome middle-aged man just along the bar had been watching through a pair of very brown eyes. He slammed his pint glass down and smacked his lips.

"That's a good pint. The eldest one, you mean? Yeah, he always reckoned he knew best. While we're at it, I remember when I was looking after the boats for hire one summer, further up the coast. He took one for a week, he did, and I trusted him to pay. Well the damn thing was towed back in within a few hours, found in the sea empty and all wet inside. And them four supposed to know about boats."

"You never told me, James," said the coastguard.

"Fat lot of good that would have done. They were always getting written about in the papers, and going to get presents from the police, and everyone saying how they were practically walking on water. Good job if they could – they were always falling out of boats. Mind you, that George – she knew about boats alright. Could row for England, that one." He grinned, cheerfully. "I liked *her*!"

"Yeah, well, the snotty one don't have to watch the coppers now," said the coastguard. "He's had thousands to spend doing up this place and Kirrin Castle and all that."

"That's as may be," put in Joan, darkly, "but I wonder who's been done out of their five bob on the way."

12

An Evening in The Smugglers' Bar

By the early evening, Anne, Julie, Jonny, Radclyffe and Dick had all returned to The Kirrin Arms, courtesy of Hugh and the launch. When George had left the island so dramatically Anne had wanted to hurry back to the mainland and call the coast-guard, but Julian had squeezed her arm.

"George has always been at home in her boat. Radclyffe isn't worried. Don't worry, Anne, old girl. She'll be OK." It was true that Radclyffe had been alternately shrugging off concerns and cornering Hugh, with whom he had seemed to have formed an unlikely partnership.

Once back in the village they had all been relieved to see Gary tied up and snarling at passers-by outside the pub.

"Thank goodness!" said Anne. "George must have arrived safely. You were right, Ju." She went to pat Gary, but changed her mind as he bared his teeth and pulled at the lead which held him to the post. In the middle of all this, George appeared from the public bar and wordlessly put a hand on the creature's head, kneeling on the concrete beside him. The dog subsided, and George looked up at her cousins in silence. Anne shuffled her feet a little and gave George a weak smile. She was looking quite puffy about the eyes, noticed Anne, watching her untie Gary and push him up the stairs in front of her.

"Oh dear, Radclyffe. Do you think you ought to go and talk to her? She needs cheering up, and I'm sure you're the one she needs at the moment. I do think that a glass of Lucozade would help, too."

Radclyffe gave Anne a straight look.

"No. She's always angry about something. Always in a mood. There's no point. I only make her angrier, anyway. I'm going for a walk until supper."

Dick looked at the boy scuffing his way along the quay, kicking stones, hands in his pockets. What did he do with himself, living in a concrete flat with his volatile mother full of resentment? What happened to boys like him? Dick knew the answer, and felt uncomfortable. If he had a son he wouldn't leave him to work things out for himself.

Once upstairs, Anne knocked on George's door, but got no answer. That wasn't surprising – she was probably exhausted after all her rowing, and would want a nice bath and a rest. That would do her the world of good. Anne turned her thoughts to supper and how marvellous it was having clever Ju as the owner of the place. They were all to have a lovely meal together in The Smugglers' Bar and it had been a *jolly* long time since Anne had had a proper grown up evening, or at least one where she wasn't the hostess; she was looking forward to it.

The children were having their meal early and could all go up to bed for a proper night's sleep before the new adventures of the morning. The grown-ups, however, would have a super evening in the bar, catching up on old times. Once they had eaten their Cap'n Birdseye Kiddies' Platter, Anne supervised her children's baths, attempted to get Julie through some Grade II violin practice, and *nearly* managed to hear Jonny all the way through the six times table. Oh dear, he was supposed to know them all the way up to the twelves by now. Julie settled down with her book propped up on her pillow. Those chummy children had stopped romping with hairbrushes and tennis racquets and had crept out of their school dorm by moonlight for some sort of picnic involving tinned evaporated milk and sardines. She read it voraciously, but felt irritated at the same time. Life was dull, and nobody did that stuff. Nobody she knew, anyway.

Radclyffe seemed used to looking after himself. He had come back from his walk, wolfed down his supper, and goodness knows what he was doing now.

As she brushed her hair and popped on a fresh blouse Anne worried about whether George would actually join them. She had looked so sad, and Anne would like to help if she could. The trouble was, helping George wasn't at all like helping the people she knew in Wimbledon. Rather like getting too close to Gary, there was the risk of being chewed, mangled and spat out.

George was feeling tired and desperately hungry after her unaccustomed exercise, and strangely in need of some time with her youngest cousin. She had been so hurt by her encounters in the public bar, so miserable at the thoughts of her beloved Timmy, she needed someone *kind* that evening. George found Anne exasperating, prissy and pointless most of the time, fussing around like a Twinkle princess, but she was unfailingly *kind*. And she had shared her past and loved her island, which really counted right now. George resolved to try her best to keep her mouth shut, be brave and join them all for supper. Julian would be there as part of the package, and that would be hard, and men were bastards, she knew. But they were family. She wound a Peruvian cotton scarf around her neck as a concession to dressing up.

*

By a quarter to eight the four cousins were seated around a polished oak table in The Smugglers' Bar with baskets of Fisherman's Scampi and plates of Farmer's Hearty Chipped Potatoes – crinkle-cut, which was a nice touch. Uncle Quentin and Yu Na seemed to have made other arrangements, which made things easier all round. The Kirrin Arms was doubtful about George's vegetarian requests, but the kitchen had managed an omelette and Julian assured her smoothly that the eggs were free-range, from Kirrin Farm. Definitely. He hastily summoned a bottle of Mateus Rosé, opened it with a flourish, and poured everyone a large glass. The curly-haired waitress hovered for a minute or two longer than needed, until Julian waved her away. She left with steady look back over her shoulder.

The cousins eyed each other slightly warily for a while. Julian asked Dick politely about his work at the Met. Dick sighed a little but put on a brave face and said it was not too bad, but really not what they might imagine it to be. He rather hoped to imply that he might be doing something important which he couldn't tell them about. He told a police joke about an asthmatic driver and a breathalyser which wasn't very funny, but the cousins laughed quite nicely. Anne looked at Dick for a minute and wondered what he did when he wasn't at work. He was looking a bit uncared-for, she thought, and a bit sad under all the jokey talk. Julian ventured his praise for George's rowing skills.

"Like riding a bicycle – once you've learned you never lose it, old girl. *You're* not like a fish on a bicycle, as they say, ha, ha! And you always loved that old boat. I didn't even know it was still there – perhaps there's still some buried treasure on Kirrin Island!"

"Yes, that was impressive," added Dick, with genuine admiration. "Just like old times."

"Aren't your arms sore? I've got some lovely Badedas bubble bath," offered Anne.

"Thanks, they are a bit," George mumbled. As she didn't seem inclined to add to that, they looked around a bit vaguely and shared observations about Julian's new decorations in the pub – fishing nets with glass floats, old oars, random portholes, vivid lobsters and ships in bottles. Anne and Dick agreed it was lovely, and George managed to sound non-committal, which was an effort, aided by her exhaustion. Julian avoided the topic of Kirrin Enterprises and filled their glasses again. George saw how hard they were all trying, and stayed quiet. The barmaid returned quickly with the wine and, setting it down, bumped a little against Dick's shoulder.

"Sorry," she said, and gave him a direct stare. Dick was just looking up from his glass when he caught the look. There was something particular, something *personal* about it. He stopped, his glass just below his lips. As the waitress moved swiftly on to the next table an excited flush crept over his cheeks. He *knew* that face! Strong and alive – insolent even – though now lined a little. The short curls had touches of grey, but the eyes were as bright and knowing as they had always been. He realised that he hadn't ever felt a surge of confused excitement like this before. Not with the typists, and certainly not with the WPCs. Dick liked it. He liked it very much. He looked around the table, but no-one else had noticed this little exchange. Julian hadn't recognised her, and neither had the others. He finished his wine quickly, and hoped very much that Jo – Ragamuffin Jo – would soon be back.

*

88

By a quarter to nine the cousins had managed to eat their meal without argument, and Julian had left to talk to Bianca about some business. Hugh, too, had left to sort out some arrangements for the next day. The waitress who had served and cleared up after their Kirrin Black Forest Gateau (which seemed to be much like the general version) had been a youngster with adenoids, which left Dick in agony. Where was Jo? She had been behind the bar for a while, but he hadn't seen her for some time. He wasn't used to wine, he felt light headed. He got up and excused himself to find the gents. He could do with a few moments to think and, more importantly, he could do a bit of exploring and perhaps find her. Anne and George were left rather uncomfortably at the table. Anne hadn't been to a pub without Rupert before, and was finding it quite a strange feeling, but a couple of glasses of rosé had relaxed her enough to stop popping upstairs to check on the twins. She had polished the pudding spoons vigorously with her paper napkin earlier, but now she was feeling rather mellow. She gave George a smile.

"I'm so glad you're here, George. It wouldn't be right without you. Not just tonight, but the whole thing. Oh dear, my glass is empty again." She looked at it in surprise. "But, George, thinking about the castle – and the island – I…I'm not as silly as you think." She stopped for a moment to brush some crumbs from the table into her hand and deposit them into the ashtray. "I know this is hard for you, George, and I know you are doing your best, but I wish you weren't so upset. It'll all be lovely, really it will. I'm sure of it. I wish you wouldn't worry."

George gave her a watery smile.

"It's alright," she said gruffly. "I'm quite glad *you're* here, actually. I didn't think I was, but I am now. Don't ask me about it, OK? Just have some more of this stuff." Julian had left them with a full bottle and George glugged out another glass for each of them. She looked a little wryly at Anne. "Come on. Let's drink it all; I need a bit of oblivion before tomorrow. But I will try again, I promise. *I'm* not as silly as you think, either." They clinked their glasses together, and Anne took a gulp. Then another. She hiccupped, and looked across at the next table where a romantic evening was clearly going on between a couple of about her own age.

"Look!" she said, wistfully. "He's gazing at her so adoringly. And he looks just like Cliff Richard. So kind and dreamy. She's so *lucky*. I'm sure *he* never asks her to sit on his colleague's lap to help a deal go through, or says unkind things about…um… Give me some more wine, please George." She stopped, and replaced her wistful look with a cheery smile. George felt quite softened at this chink in her cousin's armour of domestic happiness. So that distant husband of hers was not so perfect after all. Poor Anne. Poor Anne took an alarmingly enthusiastic swig at her glass, hiccupped again, and looked coaxingly at her cousin. Her hairband had slipped over one eyebrow like a pirate bandeau.

"George, old thing, you are my very dear cousin. Very dear. You are all very dear." Oh no, this could get maudlin, and George had enough to deal with. "This is so special, George – you and me – girls together. Um, sorry, I didn't mean girls, I meant, um, women. But I've got to ask you something. I've got to ask someone, and Rupert doesn't want to talk about it. Or about anything. Tell me, George, is Jonny alright?"

Well that was a surprise. George wasn't sure what to say. She thought about it. He was an odd little chap, certainly, but who was alright? Who wasn't? It depended what you wanted out of life. If Jonny was a strange child, well weren't they all, in their own ways? And why was Anne asking her, of all people? What she knew about motherhood could be written on a cigarette paper. Radclyffe was a mystery to her, and she knew she had lost the plot with him long ago. It made her sad, but she didn't see what she could do about it. She didn't have to answer, as her cousin was talking again, slurring slightly.

"I worry about him, George. He isn't like Dick and Julian were. He's all inside his own head and he doesn't like all the healthy, jolly things Rupert wants him to do. He doesn't talk properly and he hasn't got any friends, but I love him very much and I don't know if he is alright." Anne took two gulps and spluttered a little. "Oops. George. Dear old George. There's one more thing you could do, George, before the weekend is over. One more lovely thing." What next? wondered George. Start blow drying her hair and wearing lipstick?

"Visit your mother. Your lovely old mother. Please, please do, George. She would love it so much. Dear Aunt Fanny. Dear, dear, kind Aunt Fanny. Aunt Fanny who had us all in the hols when my own mother was…couldn't be…lovely old…" Anne was getting all wistful and silly, but George had drunk a fair few glasses of wine on top of the beers in the public bar. She reached out and took her cousin's hand, surprising herself again.

"Jonny's alright," she said. "He's not unhappy, and that'll do, won't it? That'll do for now?"

She found herself agreeing, with a sigh, to go to Kirrin Cottage the next morning.

Dick had found the gents and splashed his pinkened cheeks with cold water. He looked up and considered his own face in the mirror. It was roundish, and his hair always looked a bit messy. There was nothing too awful about it, but despite a bit of surreptitious practice he couldn't quite manage to look mean and moody. He tried to jut his jaw out, turning his head to a more flattering three-quarter view, and sighed. No – he looked as though he had toothache, and he couldn't keep it there and talk at the same time. He'd better give up on the chiselled look and think about his next move. What was the right way to handle this? He hadn't seen Jo – Ragamuffin Jo – Gypsy Jo – for so long, and having established that he was not a smooth seducer like Roger Moore or a rough charmer like Sean Connery he really didn't know how to do this.

Jo had been a law unto herself, feisty and deeply distrustful of the police, but she had also been fundamentally very decent. They had encountered her as children on the beach at Kirrin Bay, a truculent twelve-year-old in ragged shorts with her fists at the ready, daring them in her defiant Welsh lilt to throw her off the beach. George had been fuming and Dick, to his horror, had punched her hard, believing she was a boy. They had all been so superior, so territorial! They'd all sorted it out eventually, though, and Jo had encountered them several times after that, always fearless, lithe and acrobatic. They had relied on her skills more than once when danger threatened, and she had been as brave as any of them. Braver, because she had been alone. She'd gone to live with Joan's sister when her father was sent to prison. Even started going to school. Why hadn't they visited her – kept in touch? It was pretty shabby.

"But I *think*…I *think*…Jo always liked me," he mused. Liked him more than she liked the others, even. Perhaps much more. This had been one of his secret pleasures at the time, and he had thought about her more than once in the intervening years. The look that had passed between them that evening was the nicest thing that had happened to him in a long time, and had made him briefly forget his thickened waistline and his undistinguished career. He remembered them again now, though, and sucked his stomach in as much as he could. His feelings were very stirred up, and he realised that this was important. What did he have to lose? He would go and find her.

The kitchen was the obvious place to look, and once he had squeezed behind the bar and trotted off across the little hallway he found the door. This was it! Nervously he pushed it open, and there she was, standing alone at the sink, facing away from him and rinsing glasses, while a huge dishwashing machine rumbled away in the corner. He felt his face growing hot. Her trim shape was as firm as an athlete's. Just as he was wondering whether to creep away before he made a fool of himself yet again she spoke, without turning round.

"Well, now. I wondered if you'd come." Her voice was as Welsh as ever. Gorgeous.

He took a couple of tentative steps forward.

"Jo. Jo. I…er…I…um…" Damn. What was wrong with him?

"Oh, shut up, Dick Kirrin." She turned around, her eyes screwed up as she fixed him with another stare. Then she flashed him a grin and his heart lurched with something better than lust for a TV pinup. Better than anything. "Shut up and kiss me."

The dishwasher revved up and rattled.

Leaving the kitchen some time later, Dick had a spring in his step and a plan in his mind. Jo had kissed him! Him! Then she had kissed him again, causing a million fireworks to explode in his heart! What a woman! She hadn't given anything much away about herself, hadn't said anything romantic – just told him she was lodging here so as to be on hand for the breakfast shift while the resident landlord and landlady were on their annual visit to

Weston-super-Mare. He stopped walking for a moment and leaned against the wall of the hallway. Oh, my goodness! Had she told him that with an expectation that he would seek her out in the night? He trembled at the thought, with a mixture of excitement and fear. What if she didn't mean *that* at all, and he offended her? And what if she did mean that, and then found him disappointing? He didn't know what he should do about it, but as far as he was concerned Jo was the one for him. *The* one. He had to be worthy of her. Make her proud. If Julian could offer him anything, anything at all, he would take it and secure his connection with Kirrin and with Jo. This was a New Dick!

As he made his way past the unlit reception lobby in search of the stairs to his room, Dick heard a small sound. He stopped and listened. There it was again – a soft click from the back of the desk area. Burglars? Possibly. Very possibly. His mind began to race. This was something he knew about, something he could do – disarm the masked intruder hunched over the safe, march him into the bar where he would be greeted by squeals and applause, admiration from Julian and commendation from the local Chief Constable. His name would be in the papers. He would save the pub. Impress Jo.

He held his breath. There it was again – a click, and then an unfamiliar noise, a slight whirring – hard to place. The tiny lobby was in darkness and it took him a few moments to sense that although there seemed to be nobody else there, *something* was moving. Something at the desk, pale and slender. Was it some sort of animal? A cat, perhaps? Dick trod softly over and peered at the ghostly shape fluttering down. He thought again of Jo, and that kiss. That did it – he reached out and pressed the switch of the desk lamp, ready to confront an army of Great Pub Robbers if necessary. A long paper trail was unwinding like a toilet roll in the night. A Telex! A Telex machine going about its business in the dark, printing out a thin strip of letters which was hanging down and coiling onto the floor. He breathed a sigh of relief. Still, Dick was curious. The strip of paper and the accompanying soft clatter had stopped now, but there was the message, clear as anything. He lifted up the strip and ran his finger along it. 'TO KIRRIN ARMS. OPERATION T IS ON. DELIVERY TONIGHT MIDNIGHT. MESSAGE ENDS'

In a flash Dick saw it all. This was not an ordinary message. Oh no! This was something much, much more serious.

The cogs in his brain began to whirr.

13

Thoughts on a Summer's Night

Julian leaned back in the executive office chair he had installed in the master suite of The Kirrin Arms and sipped his single malt thoughtfully. Tomorrow would be tricky. Tomorrow would be vital.

Dick would do. He had scoffed his way through the Seaman's Supper with the others. He'd made sheep's eyes at the barmaid. He'd had a go at a few jokes which had fallen flat, and attempted to elaborate on the events from the Famous Past which he thought they would all enjoy. Julian had been indulgent, and Dick quite jolly on the whole. He hadn't asked Julian any awkward questions about the financial details and arrangements regarding the project. He had presumably retired to his bed to dream of Juliet Bravo or whatever it is a lonely policeman dreams of. There would be no difficulty there.

Anne was eager and willing, as far as he could tell, and Hugh had her eating out of his hand. She would certainly fuss about a few details, but they could be soothed away easily enough, as long as her tedious husband gave her the nod. Her enthusiasm was bankable, photogenic, and legendary. She would be tucked up tight in the family room with those unappealing children and her best hairband laid out for the morning.

But then there was George.

George sat up late in her room adjoining Radclyffe's and pulled a face. The pub was smart. It was clean, safe, and reasonably unobjectionable within the stupid hotel-ness of the place. Radclyffe had become pathetically and surprisingly excited about a bit of bourgeois luxury. There was hot water, there were imitation candle sconces on the wall, and a would-be tapestry canopy over the bed depicting some sort of blood sport. Like his redevelopment of the castle it was utterly without risk, adventure, heart or moral purpose. It was *fake*.

She rubbed her hands through her cropped curls and tried hard to think it through. This island had been, with Tim, the absolute passion of her teenage years. The rages and tempers, thrills and triumphs, fears, rebellions and hopes had all been utterly tied up with the place. It had been ridiculously dangerous at times, and fun, mostly. They had all known exactly what was right and what was wrong.

So what had happened? Even inside her stormy head, her world had been a privileged bubble, without regard to anyone outside. There had been a certain amount of fame, and some newspaper interviews, and an appearance on Blue Peter, but that seemed a world ago. She hadn't coped with them well at the time. On the whole, she had *hated* people. Hated anyone foreign, dirty, different and conversely hated even more the pressure to conform to the norms of her social class. What sort of a muddle was that for a rebel to sort out? As a child, these cousins of hers had won her round for a while; suppressed her spirit a bit, perhaps. But she had loathed and struggled against the girls' boarding school she had been sent to. Been jealous of that Y chromosome found in half the population, and completely confused about whether to seek it out for herself or reject it as a force of oppression. She had done both and stayed cross.

And here she was, morally disapproving of property as theft, but emotionally devastated and robbed of the ownership she had always assumed would be hers. It wasn't actually all bad – her few minutes of intimacy with a tiddly Anne had been almost affectionate. She had even softened up enough to agree to Anne's plea that they visit her mother tomorrow morning. Alright – she knew she should do that anyway, and would have gone without the pleading. And Julian? He *had* actually stopped the castle from falling into rubble completely, and someone had to, after all. But George was torn. Julian had tried, she supposed, to put the case for keeping the castle and the island in the family, but it had all been too much at once. Later, sitting at supper and talking about Timmy, Julian had been *almost* convincing. The fabric of her castle was safe; its soul was sucked out and gone.

Anne was fast asleep. Beautifully, peacefully, blissfully asleep. She snored a little, in tune with Jonny, and turned over. The hols would be alright after all.

14

Radclyffe is Nearly Caught!

Radclyffe was restless. His introduction to a different world had interested him, and his encounter with Hugh in the tunnels had been astounding. Such an idea! He lay on his bed with his big padded headphones on while his able mind worked through all the implications. Where did his loyalties lie? He had heard his mother coming back up, and her snores as she had passed out, physically and emotionally exhausted.

Radclyffe knew he would not sleep. His mother had never enforced a bed time – he made his own mind up about that, as he did about most things – and tonight wasn't one for being tucked up inside. His mind was too active, too full of questions. He knew it was happening tonight. He was streetwise enough to know he mustn't be there when anything was happening. Too dangerous –could give the game away. But he wanted to see what he could. He rolled off the bed, picked up his heavy boots and crept carefully out of his room, along the corridor, down the stairs and out of the back door.

But he was also restless because of Kirrin itself. Although used to a semi-nocturnal existence, Radclyffe had never experienced nights that were so still, quiet and dark, really dark. At home, it was never quiet. If he didn't have music playing his mother did, or the Wimmin were talking and arguing. And if there wasn't noise from inside their flat there was noise from outside; cars, music, voices, shouting, sirens.

Here the sky was big. In London, the sky and the stars were things up there somewhere, but invisible above the orange haze of street lights illuminating the smog. He'd never given them a thought. Now, though, he stood at the start of the quay by the jumble of fishing equipment, looking out into borrowed darkness and silence. The gulls were quiet, and the sea calm after the storm, just softly breaking against the harbour wall, as rhythmic as breathing. There was another sound, too, now he listened carefully. A sort of gentle jingling noise that he had noticed when they were boarding the launch earlier that day. It was something to do with the little metal things the moored-up boats had on them that made that sound when the wind blew. Radclyffe liked the multiple rhythms.

He could make out the ghostly shape of the island and its little castle across the water, on which some soft moonlight reflected. Above it stars twinkled, actually twinkled with pointy bits, lots of stars. A couple of lights on the quayside created deep shadows between the jumble of boxes, nets and nautical flotsam. Perhaps, just perhaps, there was the sound of a motor, or a faint luminescent wake on the dark waters of the bay. He peered into the darkness. Perhaps that was a light out at sea, faint, maybe flashing, maybe just one of those buoy things a long way off, rising and falling with the waves. Was the launch still there? He started to walk out along the quay.

Radclyffe was not the only person unable to sleep. Dick was restless for other reasons. How was it he had not kept Jo in his radar for the last twenty something years? He had been mad. A man sleepwalking. Could it be that after all this time

Ragamuffin Jo was interested in him? Could she possibly be the love of his life? The *actual true love*? The thought thrilled him.

And now, thanks to that encounter with the Telex machine, could it be that, at last, he had come across the big break – the one that would get him the recognition as an adult detective he had enjoyed when he was younger? Adrenaline and testosterone flowed through his veins, and his heart beat fast.

What first? Should he seek out Jo and declare himself, or would that risk it all being over in another mistaken fumble? Dick was already troubled by how he would greet Jo in the morning. Should he be affectionate, or should he play it cool? Or, horrible thought, was it all a big joke on her part? Dick decided not to decide. It was too important to get wrong.

Instead, he would try to concentrate on the other really important thing to be dealt with – the queer Telex message. What was Operation T and what was arriving at midnight? He looked at his watch and saw that midnight was only a few minutes away. If it hadn't been for thoughts of Jo whirling around his head he would have leapt into action already. He had a duty, now, a real duty to get it sorted out.

Dick got up, pulled his dressing gown over his pyjamas, and went over to the window. He turned off his light and pulled back the corner of the curtain. There were faint lights on the quayside, but Dick was looking further out to sea. He screwed his eyes up and held his breath so that it wouldn't steam up the glass. Out past Kirrin Island there were lights. One, and then, a little way out, another. They were moving across the water, getting closer to each other, and flashes passed between them.

"This is it," he thought. "Whatever it is, it's coming tonight; coming to the quayside. That's what the message means, and nothing which arrives this way, in the dead of night, is legit."

He wished he had gone back and collected that Telex message but in his excitement his mind had been distracted. Well he would go now. Nobody could accuse Dick Kirrin of not being game. He started to turn away from his window, but as he did so his eye caught a dark figure moving in the shadows towards the quayside. Dick wished he had his uniform and his night stick, but he did have his torch. Tying the belt on his dressing gown tightly, he grabbed it and rushed down the main stairs rather more heavily than he meant to, and opening the front door as softly as he could he set off towards the quayside. He didn't see or hear a stealthy figure follow him in the darkness.

Radclyffe was used to moving from shadow to shadow and the strangeness of his surroundings made him wary, made him revert to familiar protective patterns. He watched his shadow shorten and lengthen as he walked towards and past each light, flickering over and between the piles of boxes, strange equipment, nets and floats hanging up, and upturned rowing boats.

As he approached the end of the quay the lights stopped and the boxes became fewer. There was just a metal frame with one red lamp high above facing out to sea. Some sort of warning light, he supposed. Radclyffe stood with his back to the metal stanchion and let his eyes adjust to the darkness over the water. Yes, there was a light out there; no, two lights, out to sea a little, and close together. As he watched, one light detached itself from the other and started moving across towards Kirrin Island.

The sound that followed, very faint on the night air, was unmistakable even to a city boy like Radclyffe – the plash, plash, plash of a rowing boat heading towards the island. Radclyffe smiled to himself. A more romantic or historically minded observer might have thought about smuggling, but Radclyffe knew what was happening. Not quite smuggling; something more modern, and a different sort of evading customs. He smiled to himself. This seaside wasn't so different from Broadwater Farm, he thought. And it wasn't as dull as he had expected, either.

Radclyffe wasn't the only person watching the lights. Dick thought he had done well to follow the shadowy figure between the boats and lobster pots, while looking all the time at his feet in the dark. But now he was confused as well as excited. What was the miscreant doing? Criminals didn't creep up in the shadows and then walk out and stand under a light. And the boats out at sea? They must *be* boats, but one was fading into the distance, and the other wasn't coming back to the quayside. If they were drug runners, then one of them would have to come back to the quay with their cargo.

Then it dawned on him – they were going to Kirrin Island! Just like the old days! They would be hiding their contraband in the tunnels or dungeons, or perhaps even the old wreck, until they could find a suitable day to bring it over to the mainland. Dick also realised that this didn't leave him on his own to face a desperate gang of bad guys here at the quayside – he could call for reinforcements and he wouldn't die before he could see Jo again.

He breathed a sigh of relief, and felt emboldened to action. But there was still the matter of the figure in the moonlight. Dick might have thought twice about a dozen desperadoes but he was reasonably sure he could tackle a lone hand. Not head on of course – he wasn't stupid enough to do that – but if he nabbed the lookout that could lead the police to the rest of the gang. Anyway, it looked like a smallish man. He slipped back behind the last stack of nets and waited. He looked about for a weapon; a boathook or suchlike would be useful, but the fishermen of Kirrin were tidy folk.

Dick waited, hoping his breathing wasn't as loud as it sounded to himself. Eventually he made out the sound of soft footsteps approaching, though not quite from the direction he expected. Cunning, he thought. Using a different route. He held himself ready as the sound of light breathing became audible just behind him.

Dick had learned one thing on the streets of London – shouting "Stop, police!" was like firing the starter gun at the Olympics. Nothing made people run faster and he wasn't going to make that mistake, so instead he twisted round sharply and threw his arms around the torso, unable to resist a shout of "gotcha!" But the suspect was not going to give in without a struggle and within seconds the two of them got their feet tangled up in a coil of rope and fell sideways, fortunately into a pile of nets that was both soft and dry.

"Gerroff, Dick! You're half strangling me!" cried a voice that was familiar. Dick relaxed his grip, without letting go completely, and knelt up to look at the figure struggling below him.

"Jo!"

"Yes, Jo!" replied the squirming little shape. "Who did you think I was?" Dick's hands drew back as if they had touched hot coals.

"Oh, Lord! Oh, sorry! I mean, what are you doing here? I mean, I'm glad to see you, obviously, but…" Dick's voice trailed off, embarrassed and confused.

"What am I doing? Following you, you silly man. What are you doing, more like!" Jo laughed.

"Following me? Why?"

"Well, now, I couldn't sleep, I heard a noise and saw you leave, so I thought I'd join you. The old quayside is quite beautiful in the moonlight, isn't it? But I must say I was expecting something a bit more romantic than this. Is this what you do in London? Wrestle women to the ground?"

"No, I mean, yes, I mean no, I mean, sorry, I thought…" Dick realised that he was knee deep in a hole and stopped digging. "Romantic?"

"Well, what else?" she asked, pulling him down again.

Radclyffe had heard the commotion, and had instinctively looked about for somewhere to hide. But the voices were clearly not fighting, so he had warily made his way towards the kerfuffle and poked his head carefully round the edge of the boxes. His Uncle Dick and some woman – that barmaid, he thought – were lying on the nets and quite definitely snogging. Radclyffe didn't know a lot about romance, but he knew when he wasn't needed. He slipped past in the darkness, and made his way noiselessly back to his room. This was definitely the strangest weekend of his life.

15

Dick Works it Out

Dick climbed into bed and propped himself up on the pillows with his notebook. He wasn't in any mood for sleep, not on your Nellie! Life had just become exciting again! Here he was with a real woman to think about and perhaps a chance to gain a foot on the rung of the promotion ladder.

Once again he had come up without the Telex, but when he'd crept down to fetch it the strip of paper had been torn off. So whoever it was intended for had taken it – the game was afoot.

He needed to think this through – the lights at sea and the *Operation T* Telex which had juddered its way into the pub. Dick, like every copper, knew the astonishing drug-busting operation by the code name *Operation Julie*. Police officers had grown their hair long and posed as hippies to carry out observations in rural Wales. The streets were cleaner by six and a half million doses of LSD. Six and a half million doses! That was an operation to be proud of! If that could happen in a small town in Wales miles from anywhere why not here in Kirrin, with its tradition of smuggling? That would make people sit up. Julian, the Met, and most importantly, Jo.

Jo! Jo…Jo…Jo. It was like that song in West Side Story where the hero couldn't stop saying the name of his beloved – it was such a beautiful, romantic name. There couldn't be a prettier one. Having been reassured by Jo that she didn't mind being wrestled to the ground, but told firmly that that was the end of the wrestle for that night and they should go to their own beds, he had returned to his room in a ferment. Ragamuffin Jo might really be *his* Jo, and it was hard to concentrate on anything else. Being sure that she was *properly* interested in him was outside Dick's experience, and he hardly dared believe it might be so. The unaccustomed glow which suffused him whenever he thought of her was a feeling like no other, and he meant to hang on to it.

But there was serious work to be done and he had to try and concentrate. The strange message and the lights at sea could mean only one thing to a trained policeman. This whole business had to be about drugs. It always was. And you could hide a *lot* of drugs in the tunnels on Kirrin Island. He needed backup.

Dick was a careful policeman by nature. He needed to give his next step a bit of thought. He *could*, of course, try calling from the phone in the hotel lobby, but the dark figure in the shadows might overhear. No, that was too risky. He would wait until the morning and go to the Police House in Kirrin, and thinking about it, that might be a safer option. He would explain it all to them and they would call the Chief Constable. Dick realised that there would have been a few Chief Constables passing through since the Kirrin children were so regularly commended for their detecting, but any policeman worth his salt would see that this was big. His head swam with confusion, and the best cure for that was to get things written down clearly in his notebook.

He wrote down everything he had seen and heard in best Police Training Manual form, from the strangers in the BMW yesterday morning, the Telex message, to his proceeding along the quayside in a westerly direction. He was scrupulously careful about his description of the man on the quayside, though did not include all the unnecessary details about why he been given the slip – evidence, if any were needed, of the professionalism of this gang.

About the nature of the crime he could come to only one conclusion, but there was a problem. His thoughts about the possible perpetrators of this conspiracy were causing him some uneasiness. The thought that his own brother might *know* something about this was inescapable. No, Dick dismissed it. Julian was upright. He had never been the type to get himself into anything dodgy. His shoes were highly polished and he didn't need the money. It would likely be some posh drop-outs in an isolated farmhouse nearby, importing their hashish from Morocco, or their chemicals to make LSD. They would be used to the island being uninhabited and, perhaps, had even corrupted some of the builders who had been working on the castle, or the local fishermen.

But Dick found his thoughts turning back to Jo. He couldn't help it. The trouble was, he was just a tiny bit worried about Jo's possible involvement, and this tormented him. No, again. How could he be so ungallant? So mistrustful? He felt ashamed of himself at the thought, but also, he realised, just a tiny bit excited by it. Jo, who had lit up his jaded heart and made him stand up straighter, was a woman with an unusual past and a flexible attitude to the law. He hadn't told her what he did for a living, and she hadn't asked, but Dick felt ashamed of a growing worry that Jo might just know something about this strange message. Dick thought that he was in what they called a moral dilemma. Well, maybe not quite – if there was dealing going on, dealing which would put youngsters at the risk of addiction and crime, he knew what he should do as a decent police sergeant. If Jo was involved, that was her lookout, surely. But life had got more complicated since that amazing moment in the kitchen, and still more since the tussle on the fishing nets, and he couldn't bear the thought of landing Jo in trouble. What if she were to go to prison? Ten minutes ago, he had been having visions of walking her up the aisle. And then there was his own family. What if...? No. Not possible.

He gave up on the notebook and climbed back out of bed. He couldn't settle now. He paced to the window and back, and sat down hard on the seat of the rather too narrow boudoir chair. What was he thinking of? If Jo *was* involved he couldn't have any sort of a life with her, and if she *wasn't* he should be ashamed of himself for suspecting her even the tiniest little bit like this. There was only one thing he could do to sort this out – and it would take some courage. He would go and find her, and talk to her. And he would do it now.

Dick soon guessed that any staff staying overnight would have an attic room upstairs, and it didn't take him long to work out which one Jo would be in. He tapped timidly on the door, his heart knocking hard.

16

Getting Ready for a Busy Time

In Kirrin Harbour, the boats rocked peacefully, the sea was calm, the morning sun was warm, and the good folk of the village began to bustle about their business.

Dick's world had never looked better. Jo hadn't laughed at him. She had welcomed him in, listened to his suspicions, assured him that she knew nothing, and then good-humouredly kissed him, wrapping him up in her tough little arms. He thought he would die of happiness and began to hope that Jo really would be *his* Jo. First thing in the morning he would show her what he was made of.

On the landing, Julian, his Filofax firmly under his arm, gave Bianca a small wink. She returned it with a deliciously cool and steady stare.

In the corridor, Hugh and Radclyffe exchanged a glance and Radclyffe gave a small hop as they rounded the corner together and left the pub.

Upstairs, Yu Na rubbed something which smelled of jasmine and ylang-ylang into her husband's hands and whispered "You are a very clever man. Very clever."

*

The Telex machine rested – clean, dusted and innocent.

17

Anne Looks Forward to a Lovely Day

Anne awoke and hugged her knees. That was a bit of a mistake, because she had quite a headache, and the movement jarred her rather unpleasantly. Oh dear – that wouldn't do at all. It wasn't like her to have a headache. She thought back to last night's supper in the bar, her few minutes of conversation with her cousin, and the bottles of wine which had tasted so delicious. She thought she had better take a couple of Anadin just in case, and a jolly big glass of water. But Anne was never defeated for long, and had soon brightened up.

"We're off to Kirrin Cottage this morning!" she said to herself. "George is coming with us, and it's marvellous for us all to be together again!" All the unease of yesterday's look inside the castle, and George's reaction, was forgotten. Today was here and the sun would shine. They were to visit Aunt Fanny at her cottage after breakfast, then later they would all go over to the island again for Ju's special presentation. Hugh would be there, and had promised to spend some time with Jonny and Julie. He was so like his father – tall and handsome, straightforward and with such beautiful manners. And so clever, with his gift for science, like his uncle Quentin. Just what Jonny needed. She jumped out of bed and ran to the window, flinging it open. She felt very much better.

"Oh, it's so sunny, and the sea is so sparkly and blue! It's terribly important somehow, to have a lovely blue sea on the first *full* day of the holidays."

She padded into the alcove of the family room and glanced fondly at the two sleeping shapes. Julie, her brown hair tousled, her dark lashes curling on her cheeks. Jonny sucking his thumb and clutching a pair of plastic clacker balls, the strings tangled up with the Jaws shark. Oh dear, he had got them with that Woolworths gift token from Dick, but she had hidden them some time ago, as they were such dangerous things. She knew someone who had ended up with a thumbnail which went black and fell off. How had he found them? Anyway, the twins would enjoy it here. Picnics, making friends with the tame rabbits, and really getting to know their cousins.

Julie stirred and stretched for the small mirror she had recently started to keep beside the bed. Sitting up, she shoved the book with the capering schoolgirls off her pillow and onto the floor, took a mauve plastic box from the bedside table, and started to apply eye shadow to her barely open eyes. This was a new experiment. Anne was beside her in a heartbeat and Julie caught her look.

"Oh Mummy, everyone does, and it's aqua-tints – like the sea – so that's alright. Anyway, I bought it with my own Woolworths birthday token from Uncle Dick. *You* like to look nice, don't you, Mummy? You've got heated curlers and an Avon catalogue." She pushed her brows up in the middle and put her head on one side. Anne gave way once again because it would be terrible to start the day with sulks and tantrums. What would the others think?

"Just a *little* bit, darling." The pale blue smocked dress, laid out by Anne the day before, had been kicked under the bed.

And there was Jonny. Not that there was anything *wrong* with Jonny. She had a vague memory of saying something about it to George last night, but she couldn't quite remember. Anne thought it had been quite helpful, but still felt doleful for a moment. Jonny hadn't seemed very excited about the island yesterday. She sighed as the sound of the transistor radio playing 'Le Freak, C'est Chic!' from under the blankets heralded her son's awakening. At least it might help his French. Anne bent down to put her face very close to his and smiled brightly.

"Good morning, sweetheart. It's such a lovely day! Let's get dressed and have a really scrumptious breakfast." Jonny stared, fidgeting under the covers.

"*A Mars a day helps you work, rest and play,*" he muttered.

Anne cleared her throat and took a deep breath. "Hands out of pyjama trousers, darling. We're awake now". She wouldn't be repressive though. Definitely not. "Up we get! When we were children we used to open the curtains before we went to sleep so the sunlight would come streaming in and wake us up in the morning. And, of course, Timmy would leap onto the beds, and he was such a licky dog." She looked doubtful even about her own suggestion. Dogs licking her children's faces – not really! She felt a little bit *more* anxious. Surely Jonny would pass Common Entrance next year? He had such support at home. Every advantage a boy could have.

As they all got dressed, Anne wondered about George's boy Radclyffe. He was at an awkward age and rather an unknown quantity, always wandering off on his own. Obviously, he had experienced a difficult childhood, living on that terribly rough estate with George for his mother, and no father to be seen any-where. Anne had watched him with his shoulders hunched up, kicking a dropped can around the car park yesterday evening. He just *mooched*. He didn't seem to have any homework to be getting on with. He needed something interesting to do. Perhaps Hugh could find him something? It was rather a mystery how Radclyffe had come into existence at all, mused Anne. George was so difficult where men were concerned. She seemed to prefer the company of women these days. Perhaps George was...? Anne stopped herself. She must have had some sort of relationship with a man, because there was Radclyffe, and there wasn't any other way, was there?

As a counsellor, Anne had been on a course. She prided herself on knowing about the challenge of those who pursue their own individual fulfilment without regard for the limits set by society. George, she thought, had suffered at the hands of those who demanded conformity without understanding, but Anne couldn't help wondering if life was easier when people kept their feelings a bit more to themselves. Of course, she knew from her counselling groups how damaging that could be, but even so...

She ushered her children downstairs to the dining room wondering whether it was time to give the twins some advice about Radclyffe, to help them understand that his interesting colour made him no different from them. Of course, he hadn't had the *advantages* they'd had – a stable supportive family with two parents who encouraged them at every step. Well, Rupert didn't have much time to encourage at the moment, but once Jonny began to get interested in outdoor games Rupert would feel proud of him, Anne was sure. Jonny would soon take to reading and rugby, although it was a rather rough game. He'd make some friends, and they'd all have jolly times with Rupert. Camping perhaps? Anne had suggested it last summer. She had bought Rupert a gorgeous family tent with three rooms, and an awning, a special sort of hanging wardrobe, and a *super* cooking set with its own little gas burner. The folding-up washing bowl was ingenious. Unfortunately, Rupert hadn't managed a weekend off since Christmas, Julie had shrieked at the thought of spiders and earwigs, and Jonny had gone very still and white. Anne had been a little bit dubious about it herself when she had thought harder. Jonny needed to be careful of his environment – anything could set off his asthma, and a sleeping bag, even with a special liner, would certainly bring out his rash. So the tent had stayed in the loft, carefully vacuum wrapped. Never mind! Here they were back at dear old Kirrin, and although camping was all very well there was something reassuring about staying in comfort. Now a caravan might be worth looking into…

Anne, Jonny and Julie were the first to take their seats for breakfast. Anne was glad to see that there was orange Rise-and-Shine ready in a jug, its packet of powder stirred into the water. It was lovely and sweet, with plenty of added vitamin C, and both children liked it. She poured them each a glass, pleased to think of the healthy start to the morning they would have, and began to chatter about the plans for the day. First of all, there was the visit to Aunt Fanny which would be lovely. Dick and George were coming, of course, so presumably Radclyffe would join them, and she did hope Julian would have time, too. He had such a lot to do, because later on the grown-ups were going to have a conference with Julian, over on the island, where he would tell them all his wonderful plans and show them some slides.

"Perhaps Aunt George will show you just where Timmy discovered the entrance to the old well shaft," suggested Anne, "although the dungeons below will certainly be unsafe." She remembered how they had all mooed and baa-ed at that horrid, spotty-faced Edgar Stick down there. Oh dear, Edgar, who had had such a terrible upbringing with those nasty parents, might be seriously traumatised now by that experience. How dreadful! The echoes in the old passages would upset Jonny too; he was a sensitive child. She reminded the twins about the shining ingots, and that poor kidnapped little girl. They knew all about it already, of course, because she had told them lots of times. Lots and lots. But actually being here would make it more thrilling and they would certainly show some interest now. Julie and Jonny were spooning Sugar-Puffs into their mouths, and appeared not to have heard a word. Anne looked a little wistful.

She remembered the jackdaws chack-chack-chacking around the dear old tower at dusk. Then there were the rabbits – darling tame little things. Timmy was always trying to catch one, but thankfully he had never actually gained any calories from the Kirrin bunnies – just the thrill of the chase. He had always been so obedient, so well behaved and intelligent, and ready to do whatever George asked of him. Really not at *all* like Gary. Anne would choose her moment carefully to offer the dog mess shovel and the tie-up bags.

Within a few minutes Radclyffe had joined them and Anne spoke brightly to the three children.

"So, she's my Aunt, and your Great Aunt, twins! But she's Radclyffe's Grandmother of course. I can hardly believe I've never taken you to visit her – she's such a darling, isn't she Radclyffe?" The boy looked at Anne with a strange expression. He was quite an *interesting* looking boy with that tangled, curly hair which Anne thought they called deadlocks. What a funny name for it! It could do with a good brushing. He was certainly rather exotic with that earring – a touch of the tar brush, Julian would have said – but of course that sort of language wouldn't do now. That wasn't anything *bad*, of course. They had all got over that sort of silliness long ago. And some quite nice people had earrings now, even rather handsome men like David Essex.

"Er…well, yeah, sort of. Haven't seen her, really. Mum's mad at her about handing over the island to my grandfather or something." Words such as grandfather felt strange to Radclyffe, and he uttered them awkwardly.

"Then it'll be a treat for you too!"

"Radclyffe," said Julie, through a mouthful of toast, "why are you called that? I've never heard that name before."

"You'll have to ask my mother," he muttered, helping himself to more bacon. "Something about a lonely well. It's a crap name, obviously."

Julie giggled and Anne gave her a reproachful look.

18

Dick Has an Important Meeting

It was with a confident step that Dick walked up the path of the Kirrin Police House, which was set among the workers' cottages on the cliff, and rapped smartly on the door. One hand gripped the notebook in his pocket.

It was 8am and he couldn't wait any longer. This was it! Looking round, Dick had to admit that the arrangements were a bit quaint for the late 1970s, but this was a rural force, not the Met. He waited. He waited some more. He knocked again. After another wait the door was opened by a small child in a grubby vest.

"Ooh, what do you want, then?" enquired the child.

"Please tell your father that Sergeant Kirrin of the Metropolitan Police needs to speak to him on a matter of the greatest urgency," responded Dick, slipping into official mode.

"What's that then?" asked the child, slipping into removing copious blockages from its nasal passages.

"Is your father in?" tried Dick. He would have to reduce this to the essentials.

"In what? He be in bed, he be," responded the child.

"Then would you be a very good...boy," (Dick wasn't sure) "and ask him to get out of bed, please." Dick had a little less confidence than he had started with.

"Alright, keep your 'air on. 'Ere, you don't look like a police-man – where's your 'at?"

Dick was getting to the end of his tether. He had been clutch-ing his warrant card in his pocket ready to present it to a fine upstanding member of the rural constabulary. He hesitated.

"Here," he said, putting it into the child's grubby fingers, "take this up to your father now and tell him to get down here as quickly as he can because this is important." Dick enunciated every word careful and put lots of emphasis and syllables in 'important'.

"Alright, but you'd best wait 'ere," responded the child as it shut the door on him.

Dick had an uncomfortable wait. He wondered whether he should have parted with his warrant card, and where the child might have put it now. He liked children, by and large, but it had been a long time since he had been one, and he felt that children back then, even village children, used to be a lot more reliable. And, he thought, village policemen too.

He was just beginning to be concerned that the child had forgotten its task, or its father had turned over and gone back to sleep, when the door was opened by a man who looked half-awake, unshaven and very fed up. After a brief introduction, he was ushered into a front room which boasted a table and chairs, some bookshelves full of Yellow Pages, and (reassuringly) a telephone. Without sitting down, partly because the chairs were occupied with sleeping cats and old clothes, Dick began to tell his tale.

"It's like this," he began. "Last night something very impor-tant happened right here in Kirrin…"

Perhaps it took him rather too many minutes to realise that PC Dobbs did not seem to appreciate the favour and career enhancing opportunity Dick was presenting to him. PC Dobbs was starting to yawn and shuffle his feet pointedly. Nor did he appear to be pleased at the chance to work alongside the skills of an experienced sergeant of the Metropolitan Police Force of London. Indeed, he seemed disinclined to act at all. Dick was reminded of the dictum from that valuable volume *Signs of Crime*:

> Let no defeatist talk from tired men deflect you from a determination to keep the area assigned to you clear of street criminals. It may sound trite and obvious, but again it needs to be said that intending thieves are in our streets every day, waiting to be taken or deterred by active and vigilant police officers.

Well, this might not be the area assigned to him, and his findings might not be related to the average criminal on the street, but this was stirring stuff indeed. Dick was an active and vigilant police officer alright and he was determined. PC Dobbs, however, was meandering.

"I'm very grateful and all that, and I'll certainly make sure I keep an eye out, but t'ain't much to go on, is it? I mean you 'an't *actually* got that Telex thingy, and we don't *actually* know what it meant, do we? And as for them boats, well those fishermen do be goin' out at all times these days. And nights, *obviously*. All to do with the EC, they says. And if there was strange things landing on Kirrin Quay I'd know, see, 'cause I live 'ere, and everyone do know me." Dobbs hesitated. You never knew with these Londoners, and he decided that on balance he wouldn't ask Dick exactly how much he'd had to drink last night, as it was clearly more than enough, and he couldn't understand how a sober policeman could have lost a suspect on Kirrin quayside. He drew himself up, and mustered all the dignity he could in his unbuttoned shirt and tartan slippers.

"Now, don't you worry yourself. I'll be asking a few questions, just so as to be sure. And so, you just enjoy your holiday, Sergeant, and if I hears anything you'll be the first know. The very first. One policeman to another, like."

PC Dobbs smiled at Dick as he held the door open. It was clearly a dismissal. Dick was glad that when they were children they hadn't had to rely on the local constabulary to sort things out – the police, generally pretty high-up types, just turned up at the end with the handcuffs. He noticed that the few notes the constable had made were written in block capitals. Should he, Dick, go over his head to the Chief Constable of the area? He had no idea who he was.

So, having retrieved his warrant card, and rubbed it clean, he left the little police house with the calamitous thought that this opportunity to impress his superiors, to save the country from the menace of drugs, and to win Jo, might be thwarted by the inaction of a sleepy rural colleague. It might be Sunday morning but a good policeman was never off duty.

As he walked back down the path and gingerly closed the peeling gate, Dick frowned in concentration. He wasn't without friends in the right places. A few of his colleagues in the Met had moved on to the Drug Squad, and they wouldn't be so dismissive. They were men of action. Now, where was the village phone box? That, fortunately, was not a mystery – it was just at the bottom of the road, a red beacon of communication and pride of the British Nation. His paced quickened with a new resolve. However, hauling open the heavy door he was overwhelmed by the smell that announced its use as an informal public toilet, and the phone hung twisting on the metal cord, cracked and broken. Dick rattled the cradle to clear the line, then put the phone gingerly to his ear – it was dead.

"Damn! Double damn!" he exclaimed out loud. He had the biggest break of his life and he couldn't tell anyone. If only he was in London on duty, with his personal radio clipped onto his jacket, then he could call anyone, or at least any other police-man in an area with good reception. Did they have Police Boxes out here in the sticks? No, and anyway he didn't have a key and he wasn't Dr Who. There was bound to be a telephone box at McDonald's, though – out on the Kirrin bypass. He could miss breakfast at The Kirrin Arms and drive out there now. And he could try one of those Egg McMuffins.

Dick reached his Capri and roared away from the village. He found the phone box in the car park, mercifully much cleaner and fully operational. He felt in his pocket and spread all his loose change out on top of the metal coin box. One two-pence piece, four ten-pence pieces, and one fifty-pence – not bad, but he would have to be quick. Which to use first? Two-pence in case he got the wrong person? That would only last a matter of seconds, so better to start with the ten-pence. Then fifty-pence for the big story, and the others as reserves. He set the first coin resting in the slot, ready to be pushed hard when the moment came.

Holding his notebook in one hand and squashing the hand-set against his ear with his shoulder, Dick pressed the numbers on the metal keypad, much quicker than the dial version, and heard the reassuring sound of the telephone ringing at the end of the line, followed briefly by the voice of Nigel Powers – just the man he was after! Then the voice cut out and he pushed the coin firmly into the slot and heard it fall. Phew! That was always a dodgy moment.

"Nigel! Dick here – Sgt. Kirrin. Am I glad to speak to you! I was worried there would be nobody there."

"Hello, Dick. Nobody here when it's double overtime? We save up all the arrests for the weekend – keeps us in Watneys. Now, what's this all about? You want to come over to the Drug Squad?"

"No, well yes, maybe. But listen, I think I'm onto something big, really big, like Operation Julie big. But I'm in a call box and I'm out in the country so I'll have to be quick." As he was about to start his story the phone started to beep rhythmically and he positioned the next coin, fifty-pence this time. He pressed it hurriedly into the slot but it fell through and jangled in the returned coins box at the bottom. He grabbed a ten-pence piece instead, but by the time he got it to the slot the phone had gone dead. Dick started the ritual over again, and fortunately his colleague was still waiting for him.

"Nigel, look I've only got thirty-two pence left. Can you call me back? I'll give you the number." Dick looked around the box in vain – there had been a number attached but someone had stubbed out their cigarette on part of it.

"Nigel, I'll have to reverse the charges, is that alright? Hold on, I'll get right back – you won't want to miss this one." Dick hesitated briefly – reversing the charges meant using the operator and what if she was in on the plot? It was a risk he had to take. He waited while she called through; "Will you accept the charges?"

"Nigel, good, right, got your notebook ready? Here it is…" Dick started from the beginning, reading steadily from his notebook. The relief he felt, as it became clear that Nigel was interested, allowed him to draw breath at last. But he had expected nothing less. Nigel was a busy copper; he was ambitious. He was also thorough. Who owned Kirrin Island? What was Julian's company called? Dick couldn't remember, but he had the invitation in the car.

"Hold on," he said, and left the phone dangling while he scrambled to the Capri, got his key in the lock and grabbed the invitation and directions from the passenger seat, hurried back to the phone box, wrenched open the door again and picked up the receiver. "Kirrin Enterprises Limited, registered at the Barbican."

This was different. He was glad, now, that he worked for the Met. They would *do* something. Dick told his colleague about the men in the black BMW spotted on his arrival at Kirrin, furious with himself for not noting down the number. It was the new model, the 325, and they didn't come cheap, so that was pretty suspicious. He told him about the long history of smuggling at Kirrin Island, too, revealing a little of his own past as he did so.

"Wow, you know a lot. Hey, just a minute – there's a lot of Kirrins here. Kirrin Island, Kirrin Enterprises, and you're Kirrin too – what's going on?"

"It's a local name," explained Dick. It seemed his colleague hadn't made any further connections. But that didn't matter – this was here and now. Dick realised he was being eyed by a gangly teenage boy hanging around outside the phone box, trying to catch his eye and signalling towards his wrist.

"OK, Dick, leave this with me. I can't see how I can call you back at this place you're staying in – too public – so leave us to deal with it. You know I'll do the right thing." Dick leaned heavily against the door to open it, getting shoved by the teenager in the process, plonked himself into the driver's seat of the Capri, and took a deep breath. The wheels were in motion! It was like the old days again, except Dick was managing this one without Julian and the rest. Who else could he trust? He dared not tell the others, especially Anne, in case they panicked and gave something away. He just had to keep calm and wait. Jo would be amazed.

Back at the Police House PC Dobbs mused, sucking the end of his pencil. He had heard about the Kirrin children from his father, who had inhabited the Police House before him. Always getting lost in boats, and trapped on that island, and always coming up with miraculous discoveries of criminal conspiracies that made the local police pale in their shadows, so to speak. This sounded like more of the same – swarthy men, suspicious lights, and smugglers. Really, smugglers! What did these Londoners think went on down here? He knew that a few bottles might come across the quayside now and then, and a few catches that didn't get registered, but that was different.

Anyway, what was he supposed to do on a Sunday? He wouldn't be thanked for bothering Headquarters when all the senior officers were on the golf course or having Sunday lunch in the clubhouse. Smuggling was something for the Customs and Excise and he'd have a quiet word with them on Monday. That would be doing his duty, and nobody could blame him if it turned out to be a lot of baloney, which it would. In the meantime, he had important things to do; his dahlias wouldn't wait. It was the Kirrin Show soon and he was going to win this time, if it killed him.

Forty-five minutes later, Dick was sitting in the pub kitchen with Jo, having evaded his family on the way in. He was wolfing down a ham sandwich with enjoyment. It was quite the best ham sandwich anyone had ever made him.

"I can't tell you much, Jo. It's all a bit hush-hush. You'll just have to trust me." Jo flashed him a grin. She'd always liked this one, and was starting to remember why.

"Oh, Dick, what am I going to do with you? Don't go all heroic on me, now, will you!" Dick glowed as she moved in for a kiss.

19

At the Kirrin Shop Again

After they had eaten breakfast, Anne was thrilled that Julian and Dick had both agreed to join her, George and the twins. The only disappointment was that Radclyffe had just gone off with Hugh, and George didn't seem to know when he would be back. They would have to go without them both. At least Radclyffe had taken Gary with him.

Dick had missed breakfast, which was very strange. They were short of waitresses, too, because the skinny one who'd been on the bar last night had not shown up, which made Julian slightly annoyed. He was paying the staff, and they shouldn't forget it. When Dick had eventually appeared, he had looked a bit flushed and pre-occupied. Excited, even, thought Anne, which was jolly nice. Julian had attempted a pleasant talk with George over breakfast, but could not read her reactions well enough to know whether he had had any effect. She was back into her silent mode, and that was that.

Nevertheless, Anne's spirits were high as she supervised some tooth brushing and tried to find Julie's pretty smock. Where was it? In the event, they compromised on some nice denim shorts with a lovely appliqué flower badge stitched on by Anne herself, perhaps a little outgrown, and a tee-shirt with some sort of a picture of singers on it. Jonny always wore whatever Anne dressed him in, as long as it smelled right to him, and Anne herself was feeling fresh and jaunty in a flared nautical skirt with a sailor-collared blouse and some tennis shoes with little anchor motifs. Just the thing! Soon they were all ready, and waiting outside, where George, wearing a clean pair of jeans and a blue checked shirt which caught the colour of her eyes rather well, was finishing one of her strange cigarettes and looking out to sea. Anne averted her eyes.

"Julie, would you run along and see whether Uncle Dick is ready? He's gone off to write something in his special notebook, look. Over there. It's time we were off. Oh Julian, here you are! What a beautiful sweater. Is it cashmere?" She sighed as Julie rolled her eyes heavenward and slouched off, muttering under her breath. While they waited, Julian checked a few notes, and Anne tried to involve George in a chat, once she had disposed of her roll-up. The old days were very much on her mind.

"I say, George, I keep thinking of all our exciting times. Do you remember how Timmy used to bark at the waves? And how he managed to rescue our treasure map when the wind took it off to sea? I've often thought we should write a book about our adventures! What do you say?"

George grunted. "Bloody Dick, with his butterfingers. Too busy thinking about his next meal to keep hold of the thing." A book always told more than one story, supposed Anne.

"Who's talking about me? Nothing bad I hope?" Dick had hurried back to them looking rather pleased with himself. His telephone call earlier this morning must have been a nice one. He was looking quite mysterious, too. What on earth could he possibly be up to? Perhaps he was planning a lovely surprise for them all. Anne smiled as Julian began to lead them off towards the Kirrin Village Road.

"No. Let's cut across the beach and go up the path through the garden," insisted George. She didn't want Julian to decide. This was *her* childhood home, not theirs. She began to stride across the beach. Anne and Julian followed, and Dick trotted after them.

"Slow down," wailed Julie. "I've got sand in my shoes. It's horrible."

Jonny had his earphones on and clutched his pocket transistor radio, fussing with the tuning dial. They stopped for a moment. George was standing with her arms folded and her jaw thrust out and Dick was stuffing a piece of fluff-covered peppermint Fry's into his mouth. Anne looked at them all, and had a moment of doubt. Oh dear, it wasn't quite the same, somehow. Or was it? The youngsters were different, of course, but perhaps the others were much as they had always been; just older, fatter, a bit grumpier. She wasn't fatter herself, of course, because keeping nice and trim was important. She stopped and slipped her arm through Julian's. What would Aunt Fanny make of them?

"Of course!" she said suddenly. "We must pop into the shop first, and find a present for Aunt Fanny! Oh, I do hope it's still there. Children, you'll love it, and it sells absolutely everything! I suppose it might not be open on a Sunday, but it's worth a try. They sell fresh milk and newspapers, I'm sure, so they probably *can* open, by law. Please, everyone, do let's do that first."

"Good idea, Anne, old thing, though we'd better buck up," said Julian. George scowled, but turned round, and they all retraced their sandy footsteps towards the village.

To Anne's delight, it *was* still there, and they had caught it open. The window was bigger now, a sheet of plate glass replacing the small panes which had once displayed the jars of humbugs and gobstoppers. A rotating stand of postcards stood outside next to a model of a little boy with sad eyes wearing a leg brace and holding out his hand imploringly for you to put a penny in the slot. Anne put a penny in straight away, then almost skipped a little as she pushed open the door. At the till the assistant, chewing a piece of gum, glared at the twins and jabbed her finger at the notice prohibiting more than two schoolchildren entering at once.

"Oh dear!" Anne was a little flustered now. "You all wait outside, children, and I'll choose something for Aunt Fanny. George, Dick, you come and help me."

Cautioned not to talk to strangers or wander off, the youngest members of the Kirrin family shrugged and parked themselves by the bins. Julian was already walking round the outside of the building and eyeing it speculatively.

Inside the little shop the display of Star Wars plastic figures, sweet cigarettes and Mother's Pride did not look very promising. Ann remembered the creamy homemade ices and the plentiful torch batteries and useful balls of string. Instead, Crispy Cod Fries and Sky Rays looked reproachfully up at her from the freezer.

"Well *I* don't know what she wants," muttered George, putting down a copy of *Woman's Own* in disgust. "Not this rubbish." *Please your hubby with these dainty potato treats.* Why did everybody think food became some sort of a treat just by being put on the end of a cocktail stick? Pah!

"There are some flowers." Anne looked doubtfully at the improbably orange carnations in cellophane. "Excuse me, do you think you could give me some help, please?" The sullen girl shifted her chewing gum to the other side of her mouth. "We're looking for a present for a dear old lady at Kirrin Cottage – you might know her. Do you have anything she might like?" The girl stared. Then she folded her arms and narrowed her eyes.

"Mum!" she yelled suddenly, and a buxom woman in a brown nylon overall, with corns spilling over her red Dr. Scholls, appeared from the door at the back.

"Oh, hello," beamed Anne. "We're trying to find something for the lady at Kirrin Cottage – a present. What would you suggest?"

"Well I wouldn't *exactly* know," wheezed the woman. "She doesn't come in here for fancy goods. Since the mad old man walked out on her, she's kept her shopping down to a few *special* items, as you might say, and I can't sell them on a Sunday so it's no good you asking. Poor old thing. Never gets any visitors. Quite sad, really, when you think of all them years looking after her brother's kids every summer holidays and that strange daughter of hers. Coming in here all the time, they were, stuffing their faces with ice-cream. Good for trade, mind. You could get her a glow-in-the dark lighthouse key ring?"

"Er...I'll take these chocolates, thanks." Anne pushed George towards the door. She had just about recognised this vociferous woman as the girl who used to help in the shop all those years ago.

"Better make them liqueurs, then," retorted the shop woman. "Poor soul."

20

A Visit to Aunt Fanny...and Anne is Worried

Walking up the footpath to the front door of Kirrin Cottage stirred up strong memories for all four cousins. Julian had learned his leadership here, talking sense into his wild cousin and finding out how to organise, and how to succeed. He walked a little ahead of the others, taking in the overgrown shrubs and cracked cement path. He checked his watch and trod briskly.

Dick felt warm, partly because he was sweating a little after the walk, but also, he realised, because this was where he had been part of a little team, a group of cousins who had shared the same wishes to eat ice-cream, play about with Timmy, go to the island and, of course, astonish the world with their brave and skilful adventures. Julian had been in charge, for sure, but they were all on the same side – even George, most of the time. He hadn't felt that since, but he remembered it as clearly as anything, as clearly, even, as the food, endlessly provided and always celebrated. He could almost smell the scones. He couldn't quite concentrate on all that, though, because he kept wondering how Nigel Powers was getting on with organising the Drugs Squad. He wouldn't tell anyone here what he was working on, though. Not yet. He wanted to do this one without Julian taking over, and that meant keeping his head down and joining in with the family.

Anne glowed at the thought of dear Aunt Fanny. She had been like a mother, really almost *better* than a mother. Kirrin Cottage had been where Anne felt properly at home – not at Gaylands School, rather cold and unlovely despite the romping girls beloved of Julie's book, and not at the London house of her parents of whom she saw so little – but here, in the warm kitchen. They had spent so many school holidays at Kirrin while their parents had been away doing the important things that adults had to do without children. The adventures had been frightening, tests she had to pass, but to have been left out would have been dreadful. She had washed up and cooked her way alongside the others, and managed. She had been brave, too, at times. Aunt Fanny had been here then, and she was here now. George was lucky.

George kept some way behind the others, and stopped for a minute just inside the gate, which was sagging on its hinges, scraping the ground. She drew in a breath of the heathery air. The awkward, lonely life she had led as a little girl, before her cousins had come and tipped it upside down, crept back into her mind. There had been storms here, at sea, and in the house. Her father had churned up the rage she always had somewhere about her, and her mother had generally seemed disappointed. George carried her storms with her.

She jumped as she felt an arm slip into hers. It was Anne's. George scowled instinctively, but then stopped herself quickly. Anne had been sweet last night, and she might help George through the next hour or two.

"George, I want to ask you something."

"Alright," replied George gruffly. She had been thinking a bit about Jonny, and Anne's anxious face last night, and she tried to look encouraging. Anne looked encouraging back.

"Now George, it's this. Aunt Fanny will be so pleased to see you, and I just want to say please would you like to borrow my hairbrush? Just quickly, for your pretty curls? I've got one just here, in my handbag. It's perfectly clean." George's mouth fell open. Was Anne real? "And a lovely, natural looking lipstick. You'd hardly notice, but I'm sure Aunt Fanny would like to see you looking… Quick, let me; Julian is opening the door."

Julian knocked firmly several times, but when no-one answered he turned the handle and pushed the door open. Anne smoothed Julie's hair, pulled Jonny close, and gave George another encouraging look as she put her hairbrush away and they all squeezed in to the little hallway. The walls were still papered with the chintz sprigged pattern, though now it had faded and yellowed, and Anne thought how similar it was to the Laura Ashley design she had found for her own hallway just this spring.

"Aunt Fanny?" called Julian. His voice hung in the air, and they all listened. Anne looked anxious. Her poor Aunt might think they were burglars, and there was quite a strong smell in the hallway, though Anne wasn't sure what it was. Oh, dear. Aunt Fanny *should* be expecting them. They had tried the telephone from The Kirrin Arms that morning, but no-one had answered, so they had sent one of the locals up with a note to put through the door. Only George had ever been back, and not for a few years now, since the business over the island, so the arrival of the cousins might be a bit of a shock otherwise.

Julian looked at his watch; they were definitely on time. He opened the door on the right, which was Uncle Quentin's old study. It was shrouded in dust, and empty apart from a few long-abandoned piles of papers, books, and boxes – the few that had escaped the bonfire, presumably. He closed it again, and ahead of them they all saw the kitchen door open slowly. Aunt Fanny, rather bent over, shuffled out and made her way towards them with no sign of fear or worry.

"My goodness! Who have we here?" Her face was very rosy, and she smiled serenely. Anne's little sigh of relief was audible.

"Aunt Fanny! It's me, Anne, and the others. George, too. We have all come to see you! Did you get our note? *May* we come in?" Anne leaned towards the smiling old lady, who was wrapped in a reassuringly fluffy woollen cardigan, and kissed her, holding out the box of cherry liqueurs. Aunt Fanny must be getting close to eighty, and she did look it, rather. Anne was quite surprised to see that her teeth were clearly not her own, and didn't fit too well. The old lady swayed as she turned, and Dick grabbed hold of her, guiding her carefully back to the kitchen. They all followed, Aunt Fanny speaking delightedly as she went.

"Well, what a surprise, Anne! What a lovely girl you are. What a lovely, lovely girl." Her teeth clicked a little as she spoke, and she smiled up at the ceiling. "Lovely. Always lovely. Lovely Anne."

The room seemed very much smaller than Anne remembered it. Indeed, it was a bit of a squeeze for them all to fit around the farmhouse table, even after the twins had been sent outside with cups of musty lemon squash and told to explore the gooseberry bushes. Of course, they had all grown so much since they were last there. Especially Dick.

The ceiling seemed terribly low, and once they had sat down there was little elbow room. In some ways this was good, thought Anne, because the closeness seemed to fold them all together and to keep George's temper inside her. She was bristling about something again – perhaps the encounter in the shop? But, supposed Anne, even George had some consideration for her mother's feelings because although she glared a good deal, she said nothing.

"I hope you like the chocolates, dear Aunt Fanny. I'm sorry we haven't brought anything homemade. Next time I'll bring you some of my crab-apple and mint jelly. I've got heaps – such pretty jars, too. Oh, Aunt Fanny, it's wonderful to be back. Wonderful to see you again. Now you just relax and let us look after you." She rose to bustle about the little kitchen, looking for the tea caddy. George scowled in her direction, and then pointedly at Dick and Julian, and made no move to help. Why should it always be a woman making the tea? It was the same when they were young, and nothing had changed. Aunt Fanny stared into the middle distance, quite beatifically.

Aunt Fanny had always been there when they had wanted her. All those times when picnic lunches had to be made at short notice, or when all those dirty clothes had to be washed after they had been scrambling over the cliffs at night. Or at least, she was always there when Joan did those things.

Just as the size of the kitchen had changed, so had Aunt Fanny herself. Anne remembered how neat she had always been, and well presented. But now her hair, yellowish-white and straggly, looked uncombed, and the buttons of her cardigan were not done up in order. The sense of disarray reflected that in Kirrin Cottage generally. Anne searched in cupboards and on shelves for matching cups and saucers but gave up.

A few minutes later, silence gave way to the rattle of sadly chipped crockery as Anne served them all. By unspoken agreement they did not mention Uncle Quentin or Kirrin Enterprises. Julian slipped upstairs, saying that he wanted to check the cottage was in good repair, and all nice and ship-shape for his Aunt. He had produced a tape measure from his pocket, and his Filofax. They sipped the tea, Aunt Fanny moistening her dry lips with a handy glass of water which she kept clutched in her shaky hands. Anne thought she had better cheer things up.

"I say, everyone, do you remember those marvellous fruit cakes that Joan used to make?" she asked brightly.

"Ah yes," said Dick. "And I remember something else – the OBCBE!" He looked rather forlornly at his tepid cup of tea, and the space next to it which in the old days, he thought, would have been filled by a big slice of cake on a plate. Aunt Fanny was looking a bit lopsided, somehow, and although fairly cheerful was distinctly wobbly even in her chair. With some effort, she focused her eyes on Dick.

"What was that, dear?" she asked.

"Oh, once, a long time ago, Anne awarded Joan the OBCBE – the Order of the Best Cooks of the British Empire."

"And she was, wasn't she, Aunt Fanny?" said Anne. And one of the best cleaners, she remembered, looking around. Not only was the kitchen smaller, but it was also undoubtedly grubbier than when they were children. And, thought Anne, Aunt Fanny doesn't seem to go to the bottle-bank very often. Perhaps they didn't have such things outside London.

"She was a treasure, an abs'lute treasure" said Fanny. "You can't find people like that anymore. Did it all for about three-pence ha'penny. Treasure." Oh dear, perhaps she had had a little stroke?

"We were surrounded by treasure then," joked Dick. Anne managed to laugh, but this wasn't quite as jolly as she had hoped. George stirred herself.

"But you have someone who cleans, don't you mother?" This was muttered half as a question, because, realised Anne,

George really didn't have a clue. And she probably didn't approve of exploitative jobs where the working classes pandered to the whims of families like hers had been. Anne felt perfectly comfortable with the arrangement she had with Mrs. Finniston because of course she was always *terribly* polite to her and kept her well supplied with really good cleaning products. She wondered a little wistfully how Mrs. Finniston was getting on with scouring the dustbin.

"Well, I'm not too bothered about cleaning, dear. I usually spend the money on little treats instead," said Fanny, and giggled to herself, almost girlishly. Dick and Anne exchanged uncomfortable glances and George patted her pockets, her fingers fidgeting for a roll-up.

Julian, too, was surprised at the unappealing interior when he made his quick recce to see what else might form part of the Kirrin Experience. How strange not to have noticed before, he thought. He considered himself very observant usually. It would be awfully bad publicity if the media got hold of Fanny and claimed she was neglected by her famous family. They would have to spruce her up and give her some lines to say if they were going to wheel her in as a celebrity at some point. Julian had longer-term plans for Kirrin Cottage as a day trip attraction with its own entrance fee. It could only benefit his aunt, too, to have the place done up. He had some measurements and notes to be going on with.

Anne was concerned about her aunt's condition. She was getting on now, and perhaps either an Old People's Home or a companion would be the answer. The thought of her aunt in a home made Anne feel sad, despite the super facilities and sing-songs they would have there. Kirrin was where she belonged.

Quentin's departure must have been an awful shock, even though he had always been such a difficult man to live with. No wonder George had turned out to be so unique. She remembered Uncle Quentin's constant threats of corporal punishment and terrible explosions of rage. Indeed, as she thought back through her counsellor training, she wondered. Suppose he had actually been properly violent? Poor Aunt Fanny…poor George! She was sure George would benefit from a bit of counselling – but how to raise it? Perhaps a voucher for Christmas?

With Anne organising things, and being very sensitive about it, the cousins eventually mucked in and washed and cleaned and tidied everything in the little kitchen. They bustled about the old woman in her chair who looked on, bemused. The four of them didn't leave it as spick and span as dear old Joan, and Anne kicked herself for leaving her little Tupperware tub of scouring powder back in The Kirrin Arms, but it was a big improvement and they all felt better for it.

By noon they had finished and hung the dishcloths on the line. Dick was in a strange mood, Anne thought, umm-ing and er-ing to be off, and indeed had soon lolloped ahead with what was, for him, quite a trot. Julian had snapped shut his Filofax, George couldn't wait any longer for her cigarette, and Anne was presenting her children to say goodbye to their great aunt. As they made their way back, Julie muttered about horrible prickly fruit stuff in the garden and no crisps, and why did the old woman sing *Why am I only the Bridesmaid?* when they said goodbye, while Jonny gave them all a quick taste of Pinky and Perky the piglets singing *Ting-a-Ling-a-Loo.*

21

Julian's Grand Presentation

"Drat this thing," Julian said under his breath, as yet again a slide appeared upside down on the wall. Things were generally slick where Julian was involved, but usually his people managed these audio-visual extras for him. Where was Bianca? She was so good at these things. Where was Hugh when he needed him? That boy was sometimes very elusive.

Julian was alone in the Great Hall of the castle where he had put up the projector. This was his big chance, and he had to get his pitch right. Taking the slide out and turning it round, he had to admit to himself that he was more than a little nervous about George's reaction. He needed her co-operation, he really did. He wasn't too worried about the others. Dick was so hopeless with money he'd sign for peanuts and Anne had so many stars in her eyes she couldn't say no. Neither of them would know what *a percentage of the net* meant, and with luck neither would Anne's boring husband. Deals like that sounded nice and promising, but by the time the gross had been syphoned off to investors and Julian's offshore companies there might not be all that much net to have a percentage of. Not yet, at any rate. It was only fair, considering he was taking all the risks, and there could be serious money in it for all of them if things went really well. He was the only one of them with the sense to see the potential of the place. That is, the *full* potential. Once the others put their trust in him they *all* stood a chance of gaining in the long run, but they had to get through the short run first.

George, though, was another proposition. She wouldn't care about a percentage of anything if she didn't like it. She had morals and she wore them loudly on her rather grimy sleeve. People with morals like that were dangerous to Julian. She probably had friends who could storm press conferences and make a stink. That was why he was giving this presentation only to her and to his brother and sister for now – keeping it in the family, he would call it. He couldn't risk her losing her temper in front of potential investors because the bottom line was he needed George. The brave, fierce young tomboy was everyone's favourite 'character' – something that had always rather irked Julian. Be a man and face up to it, he resolved. That's what the plucky young Julian would have done.

His spirits revived as Bianca came into the Great Hall.

"Ah Bianca, my dear, do help me with this dratted thing. I know girls aren't any good with machinery but this is art and you're such an exception." She deftly pulled the tray of slides from the projector and her painted fingernails flashed as she set to work pulling out each one, checking its orientation and returning it corrected. Julian re-assessed his opinion of female technical know-how just a little – perhaps George had a point.

"And how did the family visit to your aunt go?" Bianca enquired. "You English families are so strange, leaving your old ones alone. It is no wonder they turn to drink. Mr. Hugh and I have been setting some things up, things that need doing, and I think we have done a good job. Yes, very good indeed."

Julian was reassured.

"Of course, of course. I'm sure you have everything in hand, my dear." His hand moved briefly, involuntarily, towards her bottom under the crisp dark skirt, but he consciously stopped it. This was not the moment for distractions. As if sensing his temptation Bianca turned putting her back against the table.

"And what do you make of Hugh's new friend, young Radclyffe?" enquired Julian. "They seem to have formed a bond very quickly?"

Her fingers drummed the table for a while as she considered. "They are like brothers, and Master Radclyffe is very helpful – he is a quick learner. I think we will all find him most useful."

"Like you, my dear," said Julian, moving towards her. "You are good at everything." He was swiftly out-manoeuvred by Bianca, with a smile of her big white teeth.

"Quite right," he conceded. "We must stick to business for now – the investors. You have confirmed the meeting?"

"Indeed, on Tuesday in London. They came over on the same flight as Mr. Quentin and Mrs. Yu Na. They go to London on the train on Monday to take them on some sightseeing trips – it is all organised. And when you meet you will have the whole package to show them."

"Absolutely. It's going to take some money, but when they see the whole proposition they'll see it makes sense." They would have to. Living with risk was Julian's game but this was the big one and he was in it up to the eyeballs. Nothing must fail now – or he was in Queer Street.

"Bianca, you are a genius," he said. "Thank you, my dear." The slides were in order and the right way up, the folders were ready, each with the mock-up of the brochure, some staged photographs and some artists' impressions, financial projections which were encouraging if vague, and the contracts for each of them to sign. These lay in neat order on a side table ready for Bianca to give them out. The big chairs formed a half circle around the screen which stood on the dais at the end of the hall. This was it.

Hugh had really put the launch through its paces, and as a concession had let George have the controls for a while as they had circled the island, scudding across the tops of the waves and skirting the rocks. George had had to admit to herself it was thrilling. You didn't need testosterone to enjoy it. By the time they arrived at the island her mood had lifted.

Hugh led the group into the Great Hall, and Julian noticed with some pleasure that they were looking rather exhilarated (or in Anne's case, flustered). Julie seemed quite cheerful, and Jonny was re-tuning his transistor radio. Dick was looking particularly alert and restless, pacing around already, and inexplicably looking at the fittings, and up the chimney in the big fireplace. That made a change – he usually headed for the nearest chair. Radclyffe stood with his hands in his pockets and his eyes half closed, looking thoughtful. Julian couldn't see George, though. Damn.

"Oh, how lovely, Ju!" exclaimed Anne. "Everything all ready for us. I must say I'm excited!"

"Just like old times," said Julian, gesturing to the table covered with a gingham tablecloth and laden with a variety of sticky and nostalgic looking things to eat. He'd had his people scouring the junk shops for old tea sets and napkins. Nobody used that old stuff anymore, and it went for pennies. In the back of his mind Julian wondered if he had spotted a new profit centre. Could he create a market for this old junk and get in first? Well Laura Ashley had done something like it with new "old" versions covered in chintzy stuff. He could trawl around for the old tat people would be glad to get rid of. What would he call it? Retro? Too much like rockets – too Thunderbirds. Vintage? A bit like wine, but it *might* do, at a push.

"Help yourselves," he said. "I want this to be just the five... er four...of us together. I want you to see everything first. You are the important ones here. The plans are terribly interesting. Er, where's George?"

"Oh, don't worry, Ju. She came over on the boat with us, but she's taking Gary for a run around the island first," replied Anne. "She was looking quite...well, I'm not sure how she was looking. She'll be here soon enough. We may have a changed a little bit, Ju, but none of us would want to miss this." Her smile got just a little bit brighter. "It'll be super to be together for your grand presentation and George will understand once you show us all your lovely ideas. Your clever Hugh has been talking her round – and that strange boy of hers. Aren't they such a lovely pair!"

"I do hope so, Anne," said Julian. "I've put such a lot of work into it." And money, obviously. The door opened noisily and George's sturdy figure stood looking at them all with a steady gaze. Julian employed all the charm he could muster.

"Ah, George, you're here. We couldn't start without you, old thing!"

It began well enough. Hugh, after a few instructions from Anne, removed himself to entertain the three youngest family members outside. The twins had looked doubtful, but Hugh was able to entice Jonny by waving some new batteries for the little transistor radio which lived in the boy's pocket and had become rather faint. Hugh had also got hold of some bottles of Cresta, three packets of salt and vinegar crisps, and three Caramac bars, which clinched it. Julian hadn't wanted Anne distracted from the important part of the visit.

145

Julian had got Dick and Anne to send him some old snaps and newspaper cuttings, and they were delighted to see their childhood selves magnified on the projected slides in pastel tinted oval outlines, like David Hamilton portraits. Anne's hair looked so soft and pretty, she was glad to see, and George's eyes so clear and direct. Dick looked slim and jolly, and Julian very grown-up for a child. Best of all, darling Timmy was there, too, with his smiley expression and his tongue hanging out. Not very much like Gary at all.

"Well, that's how it was," said Julian. "Weren't we all rather wonderful! But this is 1979, so now for how it will be…"

At first, the projected map of Kirrin Island didn't look any different, apart from several bright little captions dotted around, and before they could read any of them Julian nodded to Bianca who moved to the next slide.

"We all love Kirrin Island, and of course it is a very special place. *Very* special." He nodded to George. "It has to be saved, but to do that we can't keep it in aspic. Times move on. If we tried to keep it all to ourselves that would be very selfish, and I think you will all agree we were never selfish, but generous, friendly, and kind to others." He remembered the way they had dealt with some of the people they had encountered at fairgrounds, circuses and kitchens, but decided not to dwell on these inconvenient memories.

"So, it could become a nature reserve," mumbled George. "Rabbits and sea birds."

"Ah, but we can do better than that. Much better. We can, indeed we *should* let the wider world enjoy our adventures, and have a little taste of the fun we were lucky enough to experience." Was he laying it on a bit thick? He had to give it his best shot. It was time for the artists' impressions, and these began to flash onto the screen.

146

"Kirrin Castle! Now, we have already seen how beautifully this has been rebuilt, of course, but as you can see it will become the central focus of a much bigger and very exciting project designed to provide a range of holiday options and facilities for day-trippers and those who want to stay and get to know the island a little better. Er…that is, for interested visitors and fans of our adventures." He remembered George's contempt of day-trippers, with their abandoned orange peel and sandwich wrappers, and moved on hurriedly. "First – holiday chalets. Four simple but enchanting cottages here on the island for families to enjoy together, to add to the four renovated coastguard cottages on the mainland." That shouldn't go wrong thought Julian, although they would be a little squashed together, just down from the castle on a flatter piece of land which he had had to utilise to the full. He cast George a sideways glance. She was inscrutable.

Anne, however, was looking as enthusiastic as he had hoped.

"Oh, what a lovely idea!" she cried. "I love the little flowery curtains, and the darling shiny door knockers. So much nicer than those horrid Butlins places."

"That's the idea, Anne. And, to make life easy for the mothers," here he flashed his best smile at her, "meals and picnics from Joan's Kitchen!" The next slide showed a jolly fat lady in a booth with a stripy awning. Julian had found it on a postcard for a nearby seaside resort and "borrowed" it for the occasion, making a kind of photo-montage with the image cut out and pasted onto one of Kirrin Island, then carefully re-photographed. It had a warm and cosy feel, he hoped. He shot a glance at Dick, who could usually be relied on to endorse sausage rolls and pastries of all kinds. Dick, however, was looking very distracted, jiggling a knee up and down and glancing at his watch.

"Anything for vegetarians?" muttered George. Julian didn't know how seriously to take this; she surely couldn't expect every fussy eater to be catered for on an island! He moved on rapidly.

"The Kirrin Island Shoppe, just by the harbour. Just a tiny little place, but with gifts, souvenirs and T shirts, so that families can remember happy times with the kiddies and take some Fanny's Fudge back for their friends. I'm thinking ingot keyrings, mystery board games, framed and signed treasure maps? Notebooks with a little picture of us all on the front? Jigsaw puzzles? I'll bet you will all have ideas."

"Well, here's an idea – ethical sourcing." George was trying quite hard, and Julian wasn't sure how to judge the gleam in her eyes.

"I can assure you, George, that none of it will be produced by slaves working in sweatshops in Hong Kong. I give you my word." Julian had foreseen this and could respond honestly – he was negotiating with sweatshops in Birmingham. He cleared his throat. "And, of course, a lovely Adventure Picnic Area. Kirrin Island is dangerous and we must keep our visitors safe. Our insurers won't want children wandering off and falling down a well or off a cliff." The publicity would be awful.

"Which places are the main no-go areas?" enquired Dick. He was looking really interested now.

"Er, well, not entirely sure yet, Dick. It'll depend on the inspectors and the insurers." Julian was puzzled. They needed to get back into the swing of his presentation.

"Julian, what else won't they be allowed to do? These *trippers*?" enquired George. The gleam had grown more intense, and this time Julian caught it and felt the beginnings of a sweat prickling his Gieves and Hawkes shirt. Damn.

"What they *will* be able to do," Julian responded smoothly, "is see the animals, in…Pet's Corner!" He juggled with the next slide, which showed a mock-up photograph of a pair of sweet six year olds drooling over some overfed domesticated rabbits clearly borrowed from a pet shop for the occasion, the hutches of hamsters visible in the background.

"WHAT! I'm trying, Julian, I am, but I'm not having anything in cages. Animals have rights too, or at least *I* think they do. If you think you can…"

"George, old thing! Look at the rabbits – they are perfectly happy! I wouldn't want the dear little things to suffer any more than you. And anyway, it's the best we can do. Our insurers were worried about the public safety issues of having wild rabbits roaming about – myxomatosis is rife, apparently, though not on the island as yet. There was a suggestion that we gas them all, as a precaution. Of course, I was horrified, George. Horrified! This way we save some healthy ones, and the children can cuddle them."

"Oh, George, surely you can see that will be nice," said Anne, a bit timidly. "I know you always wanted the rabbits to be safe. You wouldn't let even Timmy chase them. This way they'll have plenty of food and nice soft beds. But, Julian, you'll have to make sure the children wash their hands afterwards."

"Quite right, Anne. It's always sensible to talk to a mother. Bianca make a note of that." Was he laying it on a bit too thick? A glance at George gave him a clue. She was shaking her head slowly.

"No. You can't keep animals cooped up like that," she said. "I won't have it. I'll report you to the RSPCA…I'll…"

"Of course not," Julian explained calmly. "I don't want to coop them up. At night they'll have nice runs, big ones, so they can be practically free-range rabbits – and naturally rabbit pie won't be on the menu. Joke, George, honestly! I'll have their well-being at heart. Trust me."

*

Out in the castle courtyard, Julie was chewing her Caramac bar and talking to Radclyffe. They were all sitting down on the grass while Hugh went off to get something out of the Portakabin.

"D'you think we're going to light camp fires or something? My Mum goes on about all that stuff. Camping and getting made prisoner in places and washing up plates in streams – you know the kind of thing."

"Not really." Radclyffe tried to look bored. These were stupid little kids and he was stuck with them. "I haven't done any of that stuff."

"Nor us. What's your Mum like? She lets you do anything, I've seen her. I wish my Mum would. Like I said, she goes on about caves and cycling and things from when she was a kid, but all I ever get is books and dolls and sewing stuff. I got Tiny Tears on my birthday, with nappies. Not even Sindy. *And* I have to call her Mummy, not Mum." She looked disgusted. Radclyffe was quiet for a minute.

"Yeah," he said at last. "Yeah, she lets me do anything. It doesn't matter what I do. It doesn't matter at all." He uncoiled himself and scuffed off after Hugh. Jonny looked up from his Cresta.

"May the Force be with you," he said, very seriously

Inside the castle George was quiet for a moment. Seething, but quiet. Julian went for his *pièce de resistance*.

"So, what about you…er, us? Where do we fit in? Well, as we have seen, there will be lashings of everything, all designed to make perfect family visits, but for *you*, it will be completely free, any time you want to visit and share your fame with the visitors! You can bring your families as well, subject to availability and

150

a few special conditions, of course." Julian looked particularly at Anne. Entry prices could be considerably higher when a famous family member was on the island. More still when they were making proper celebrity appearances. The details could be discussed later, after some more inducements, and as part of closing the deals. There would need to be a lot of visits, and they would need to be carefully staggered to cover all the peak holiday times. First, he needed to get on with the nitty-gritty.

"So, what about your rewards? Your special involvement in this wonderful opportunity? Well, this project is going to be a tremendous success, and we are offering you a chance to enjoy a real return on your co-operation. That is, a share of the net profits for each of you!"

The gleam had become a menacing stare.

"And what do we have to do in return?" George's tone was quite even. "I can't imagine you are handing us a present, Julian. Or have I got you wrong?"

"Well, there'll be a few formalities. Er…papers to sign, image rights, and so on," said Julian. "And some personal appearances, talking to specially selected guests, endorsements, photo shoots, that kind of thing."

"I'll endorse the pies," joked Dick. He had started to concentrate on what Julian was saying. This was sounding good. It would be something to tell Jo. Something to be proud of. His mind raced ahead – when all this was over, and the police had rounded up the perpetrators of whatever was going on and revealed Dick as the saviour of the hour, Jo could be involved in Kirrin too. Why not? The others still had not recognised her, but if things went well for the two of them they soon *would* know. He wondered how the Drugs Squad was getting on with their investigations. It would be softly-softly for now, while they

151

made their observations and gathered their evidence. He looked up at the screen, which showed an old photograph of the ingots they had found in the dungeons.

"Oh Julian, it all sounds wonderful!" Anne was starting to feel excited. Perhaps it was time she was her own person, even making her own money. Rupert might really *notice* her then. Julie would be proud, and Jonny might be induced to ask her about her famous past. George was horribly silent. Her finances were direst, but...

Julian took his chance. Might as well get the whole lot done. He wanted to leave them with a sense of fun and thrills after the talk of contracts, but he knew his ideas might not be appreciated as such by everyone.

"Now, I know this is all very exciting. But there's more! Jolly thrilling things for children with a sense of adventure. See what you think of this." The next slide dropped into view. "Tunnel Tours. Exciting tours of the dungeons and tunnels under the castle. Well, a little part of them, obviously. Mystery! Danger! The lights may go out suddenly. You may hear strange sounds and see torches in the distance, and sinister men glimpsed down side tunnels!" Dick looked startled for a moment. Julian went on. "Actually, we've made the dungeons safe and dry, but they can still be made to *look* damp and dangerous again. Of course, it can't be *too* exciting for the little ones. Hugh will give you a tour if there's time, and explain our vision. I haven't been down there myself for a while, but he is getting to grips with the whole tunnels thing."

"Oh, goodness! It's terribly gloomy and frightening in there. What if the children stumble in the dark?" asked Anne.

"Oh no, I've had electricity installed, and they won't stumble because, once we have all the necessary, er, business side sorted out, they will be on little trains."

"ON TRAINS!" spluttered George. "In my tunnels! You just can't!" George's use of the word 'my' was irritating Julian.

"I'm sorry, George. I'd be with you all the way, but Anne is right. Only Quentin ever knew where they all went, and when Fanny burnt his map that was that. You know how disorganised he was – it was the only copy. Hugh has been exploring, so we're alright to a certain extent, but it would take years to sort out the rest. We can't have people wandering off into the tunnels, obviously. They might get lost, or find something they shouldn't. The health and safety people won't have it. They must be strapped in at all times."

'Boat Rides' was the next slide showing a smiling group in a little rowing boat. It was everything the Five had enjoyed. Utterly charming, with a blue sky, fluffy white clouds and jolly seagulls in the background. A small child in the photograph was clutching a little oar while his sister enjoyed an ice-cream. Their parents beamed at them, the mother waving a hanky. You could almost hear the cry of *ahoy*! Anne drew her breath in sharply.

"Oh, Julian, that's a sweet picture, but it's terribly dangerous, surely. Think of all the hidden rocks and strong tides around the island! You can't let little children row boats like that." But Julian was as smooth as butter.

"Oh, no, you needn't worry at all, Anne. You see the boats are on a special sort of track, just under the water. Well, they will be, once we have a few more funds. One of my people has been to Disneyland, and he says they can make it seem just as though they are climbing big waves and about to get soaked, and then tip them out at the end, without them even getting wet. It's terribly clever."

"Little tracks. You mean they won't even be in boats?" asked George.

"Oh, they will. In boats, but not floating."

"In boats but not floating?"

"Certainly not! My goodness, George, you know what these rocks are like! Think of the insurance pay-outs if anyone got drowned! Er…and the terrible anguish it would cause, of course. We can't have that." He risked another glance at his cousin. Her eyes had almost disappeared beneath her brows. She spoke tightly, through clenched teeth.

"Then it's a travesty. The whole thing is a complete travesty."

This wasn't going quite to plan, but Julian knew that George objected to everything on principal. She hadn't actually shouted yet, and he was pretty hopeful she could still come round. He had always made her see sense in the end, after all. Things could be worse. He took a deep breath and continued, the cheery note in his voice a little strained.

"And now for the big treat – in the evenings we have something for the grown-ups. The Medieval Banquet in The Great Hall!" Julian displayed the artist's impression of merry revellers all quaffing from tankards, served by maids and wenches in colourful costumes. This was a bit of an extra, but an important one. The ancient heritage of the castle offered too good a chance to add an extra demographic to the pool of potential customers, and the ingots had been ancient, after all. He had researched a castle near Bristol that did a roaring trade like this. "And for us all, tonight, a chance to be Kings and Queens. Tonight, we can all dress up for our own Kirrin Island Banquet. Bianca has collected a whole set of costumes in the games room, just next door to this one – men's, women's and children's. This evening, when we're back here again, everyone can go and choose some clothes and get dressed up! There is a rail of costumes there and you can take your pick!"

154

Dick's eyes lit up – beer, food, fame and girls in lovely blouses. Could he really come and be part of this for free? It was *almost* too good to be true! Then, in a flash, he remembered Jo, and thought again. She was better than silly girls in blouses any day. Anne's eyes shone at the the magnificence of the scene on Julian's slide. She thought of them all dressed up in this wonderful hall. Julie and Jonny would look sweet, and she could imagine the gay laughter and cheery back slapping so well. She turned to George encouragingly. There weren't any caged animals or little boats on tracks here. But George wasn't smiling.

"What," said George, her voice dangerously low, "are they wearing?"

Julian looked again – perhaps the blouses were a little revealing and the angles at which the wenches leaned over the tables did emphasise that. But this was a 1979 version of feasting and fun. It wasn't The Benny Hill Show – much more tasteful – but the Dads were entitled to something special to look at.

"Traditional costume," he offered. "I assure you, George, it's all very accurate. Very historical." He knew this because they were largely copied from the Ladybird Book of Kings and Queens, with a bit of artistic license here and there.

"Traditional? Julian, it's crude, sexist and chauvinistic. I'm not standing for it. Do you know what women have to put up with when they wear this kind of stuff? Have you any idea?"

"But they're being paid." He looked for support to Bianca, and then to Anne, who was looking confused. George's legendary temper, so loved by children round the country in the past, rose like a volcano and erupted all over Julian.

"DON'T you *dear George* ME. I'm not some medieval peasant. Those are MY dreams and memories you're stealing, like you stole MY island. You can stuff your bloody banquet, and your boats that don't float and trains that go down tunnels. Stuff them all up your male chauvinist…"

She stood up, her big chair falling backwards with a huge crash which echoed around the Great Hall. Gary jumped up, and followed her, feet pattering, as she stormed out through the great doors leaving behind her a stunned silence.

Outside, George trampled through the twins, who were sitting in the castle courtyard huddled round Jonny's radio, and set off down the hill at some speed. Julie wailed as her crisps flew around her, and Jonny gripped his transistor tightly.

"*Nice to see you, to see you, nice.*"

Hugh and Radclyffe appeared from round the back of the castle, and began to follow her, but they weren't quick enough.

"It's worse this time. She's taking the launch!" Hugh shouted through the castle doorway. Everyone jumped up and rushed outside to see the Pride of Kirrin, with George at the helm, shooting out towards the sea, prow up, leaving behind a huge wake which splashed white among the rocks. They stood dismayed as it quickly disappeared around the corner of the island.

It didn't take long for someone (perhaps Dick?) to utter the words: "Right. So what do we do now we are trapped."

22

George has a Plan, Too

Leaving the island at speed in the *Pride of Kirrin* George considered stoving a hole in the bottom of the boat and leaving them all stranded. But as she crossed the water, and, she had to admit, enjoyed the power and control of the launch, she breathed properly again, and mellowed.

Mellowed and planned. Arriving at the quayside in an absurdly short time she stood and looked at the boat for a while. Now both the boats were on the mainland – her old rowing boat, so leaky and loved and worn, and this new, shiny, launch, a seemingly unstoppable power which everyone found thrilling. She, too, found it thrilling, but that felt like a betrayal. Boats, dogs, islands – why couldn't things stay the same?

She headed straight off for Kirrin Cottage, with Gary trotting along behind looking unusually alert, as if he sensed that something was afoot. A plan churned around her head as she walked determinedly. She could just boycott this ridiculous evening. Just stay out of it. But George was a woman of action, and a protest by absence was not her way. No – if she was going to this banquet, this travesty, she wouldn't be going alone; her mother would be coming too. That would give them something to think about. Her appearance would rattle Quentin hard, and between them they would do their utmost to wipe the superior

look off her father's face, tell Yu Na a few things about her husband, and make Julian see once and for all that she was not going
to take his schemes lying down. Women had to stick together.

Once she got to Kirrin Cottage, she found her mother
excitable and flushed – and absolutely game for making a guest
appearance. Delighted, even. She was moving reasonably well
with a walking stick.

But when she got back to the quayside the launch was gone.
Her own boat wasn't fit to use with her mother on board.

To her dismay, none of the fishermen relaxing in The Kirrin
Arms could be persuaded to leave their cigarettes and beer to get
back to their boats and start work again, nor would they let her
borrow a boat of any kind. What was wrong with them? That
would never have happened when they were here as children.
She stomped out of the pub and paused, looking out to the
island. There was her castle, all dressed up for another round
of fakery. Damn! Her stash was damp, and the lighter wouldn't
catch. She flicked it a couple more times, thinking. This wasn't
the first time George had had to solve this problem of being on
the wrong side of the water. A grin spread over her face – there
was a way; there was a way indeed – and that, of course, was the
tunnel from the cottage. The tunnel that went from her father's
old study all the way under the sea to the dungeons of the castle.
It wasn't actually that far, but was it still open? And if it was,
could her mother manage its rocky path? It had to be worth
a shot.

Outside the castle, there had been considerable consternation
among the cousins. George had left them stranded on the
island, and no-one seemed quite sure what do. The children
had shrugged and moved off round the back of the castle. Jonny

had improbably produced some matches from his pocket, which had made Radclyffe grin at him, and they decided to try lighting a camp fire. There were some bits of paper in the Portakabin which might do, and the sweet wrappers, and right now, just for once, no-one was looking their way. In front of the castle Anne was fretting.

"Oh dear, I don't *think* she'll just leave us here, Julian. I do hope not, anyway. I talked to her last night, and she was actually quite sweet." The others looked startled. George, sweet? "Well she was," continued Anne. "I expect she'll be back soon, but we will have to make some plans, won't we, Ju? Just in case? I can't have Jonny upset – it can take him days to get over anxious situations. We were going to go back to The Kirrin Arms soon, weren't we, so we could have a little rest before the Banquet? The children really need that, Julian."

"Hmmm," said Julian, more annoyed than he was letting on. Trust George to mess things up, just when he was getting the others willing enough to throw their lot in with his project. "Bianca? Hugh? What do you reckon?"

Dick looked out to sea, anxiously. This was more serious than a bit of inconvenience. Suppose Operation T was steaming ahead in unknown ways, and they were all in danger of confronting a dangerous gang, possibly heading for the island right now? Would he be able to overpower the gang members and lock them up somehow? It had never seemed that hard when they were kids. Or suppose they were all stranded here through the night? Rescue by the Drug Squad was not what he had planned.

"Of course not!" exclaimed Anne, shuddering. "Perhaps we could signal to the mainland with mirrors, or something. Only it's not really very sunny anymore." She put her hand above her eyes, sailor fashion, and looked around. "Oh goodness, I think someone's on the island – apart from us, I mean. I can see smoke! Quickly – it's behind the castle, where the children are. Julie! Jonny! I'm coming!"

On a charred patch of grass fifteen yards away sat the three children, grubby, smeared in chocolate, poking a heap of smouldering paper and greenish twigs which sent up a thin spire of smoke. Radclyffe was lounging on the ground behind the twins, smiling in a lopsided way. Julie was intently building more twigs and pieces of bracken onto the pile, fascinated and absorbed. And Jonny? Jonny was laughing in sheer, unadulterated joy. Laughing and laughing with his hand waving in and out of the smoke.

"*Central heating for kids!*" he yelled. "*Central heating for kids!*"

Anne stared. Then, within a heartbeat she started forward, ready to save her children from burns, smoke inhalation, dirt, and danger. Her hand stretched out as she hurried towards them, handkerchief flapping. All three looked up. Radclyffe's wary expression returned in a flash, and he sat upright, his reflexes ready. Julie's eyes went heavenward, her mouth turned down, and Jonny stopped laughing. Stopped completely.

Anne stopped, too. She looked at the little scene; the smoke smelled of bracken and grass, and she breathed it in, first unwillingly, then deeply. She took in the drooped shoulders of Julie and the stiff look which had come over Jonny's face. Without a word, she walked forward and knelt down on the grass next to the twins.

"We were sending signals," said Julie slowly, looking down at her efforts. "Like you did when you were a child. Signals to get us rescued. I don't think they are very good ones, though."

There was a silence. The smoke spired up thinly. Anne put her handkerchief in her pocket and spoke quietly.

"They are very good signals," she said. "You are good at this. It's hard to light a fire when you're not used to it. It was a great idea to send signals." She paused. "Next time, I'll find you some marshmallows, too. You can toast them on sticks."

Julie looked puzzled. She glanced into her mother's eyes, and slowly smiled.

"Thanks, Mummy. Mum."

"*Goodie, goodie, yum, yum,*" said Jonny. Then, very softly, "Yeah, thanks, Mum."

Radclyffe watched Anne wrap her arms round the twins as they all looked at the tiny flames glowing on the ground. The rescue signals. Without a word, he leapt up and slouched off down the hill.

Within a few minutes Dick, who had been scouring the waters around the island, gave a yell.

"I'm pretty sure that's the launch! It's coming back for us! You were right, Anne. George must be coming to take us back to the…no, wait, it's not George. Blimey O'Reilly, it's Jo! Jo is coming for us!"

Jo had seen George arrive alone in the Pride of Kirrin, and knew enough of George to guess what had happened. Never daunted herself, Jo had no doubt that anything George could do she could do too, so she had jumped in and set off.

She was the toast of the stranded Kirrins as she slowly brought the launch alongside the jetty. They cheered and clapped; Dick most of all. He hugged her, and they sat very close as she drove them all back.

The journey from island to shore was a matter of three minutes at the most, and soon they were all back at the pub and in hot baths, getting ready for tonight's grand banquet. Anne had been astonished to see Dick slip his arm around the barmaid as she drove the Pride of Kirrin so expertly. What was going on *there*?

Julian and Bianca had some last-minute arrangements to see to, and had stayed on the island to prepare the hall, lay out the costumes, sort out the music and instruct the staff. Hugh was soon busy ferrying cousins, cooks, photographers and food onto the island. Radclyffe had stayed on Kirrin Island when the others had gone, and Anne hadn't been able to persuade him otherwise. He'd said he had a job to do, whatever that meant.

George was not in her room, and neither was Gary. This made Anne rather concerned. Feeling refreshed after her soak, and wearing a sensible pair of slacks for the imminent trip back to the island, she knocked on Dick's door; there were a few things she wanted to discuss, and now seemed like a good time. There was a little scuffle before Dick answered, opening the door slightly, and putting his head out.

"Oh, Dick, sorry," said Anne. "I suppose you've just got out of the bath. It's just that I wanted to ask you about something. About in the boat earlier, when you…you know. Your arm and… the lady driving us. Only I was thinking it might be Jo. It is her, isn't it? I recognised her on the launch." Anne put her arm out and touched Dick's. "Are you and she…um…? Only she was jolly decent to us in the past, and so I just thought I would say… I mean I'd just like to say it's a jolly good thing and I'm…" Anne didn't know what to say, but Dick caught her kind intentions and grinned.

"Yep!" he replied. "It's Jo alright. I knew it was her in the bar yesterday, and we…er…got talking. Wasn't she amazing, turning up on the launch, just when we needed her? Just like Jo – she's quite a woman!"

Anne gave him an awkward hug as best as she could with the door in the way, and retreated to her own room. The twins had asked her which was the most dangerous adventure from her past, and she was looking forward to telling them about the time they were held prisoner in the same house as a violent escaped convict.

Back in his room Dick paid a lot of attention to shaving, splashing on plenty of Denim. As they had made their way back to the pub Jo had told him she was serving at the banquet and had a peasant blouse to wear and did he want to help her lace it up? Dick did.

23

A Marvellous Banquet!

Julian felt pretty confident that his banquet would be the most splendid event ever seen in the hall of Kirrin Castle. He was almost certainly right – the original castle had not actually been the home of a noble prince; more likely a hideaway from pirate adventurers, or perhaps even a home *for* them. Pirates would not have needed much show – rum, women and a bit of song would have been enough for them.

Tonight, half of the hall was bedecked with banners hanging from poles and strung across from wall to wall. The tables, if not quite groaning, still looked impressive with goblets, wooden platters and jugs of wine. Two giggling teenagers in long dresses bustled about under the direction of Hugh and Bianca, instructed to "make everyone feel special." They seemed a little uncertain whether to go for reasonable efficiency with the wine jugs or drama-school versions of wenchy banter. Tonight was a trial run, of course, though there was a photographer for publicity stills, and that would be a big plus. The costumes had by and large been part of the package from the Camelot stuff. When he had first seen them, Julian had thought kingship became him, but out of calculated deference to his brother and sister he had declined a crown – although he was the eldest – and appointed himself a noble earl instead. Julian had quite often speculated about the Middle Ages: deference, command, no unions, no civil rights – ho hum. Bianca had found a rather startling purple gown and a high pointed hat, which she had deftly adjusted to give a better fit. Hugh had managed to look elegantly confident in tights. Radclyffe, too, had joined in with the spirit of the evening and made a rather fetching young squire.

Yes, thought Julian, soon the sound of merrymaking would fill the hall, and his brother, sister and hopefully his cousin (the publicity shots *should* be so much better with her, if she was in a reasonable mood) would look the part and enjoy it. Quentin (and Yu Na, though she was useful only to keep his old uncle on track) would provide an added layer of character and interest. It was a pity the grander side of the catering hadn't started yet – it would have been a good chance for a dry run at the ox roast – but the expense for so few could not be justified or managed, and if people roasted pigs at village fetes, he supposed they could manage it in the vast fireplace of the Great Hall. For now, a more manageable menu was being provided from some of The Kirrin Arms staff, together with the wenches.

Right now, there was a more immediate problem to think about – would George come? Anne had talked her round before, and although George was a hothead with strange ideas she was, in the end, presumably still good-hearted, and certainly still his cousin.

Anne was first to enter the Great Hall as a guest, with Julie and Jonny looking itchy and embarrassed in their costumes. They stopped at the doorway for the photographer to arrange the little trio, and then take half a dozen shots, waiting each time for the flash unit to re-charge, in the hope that at least one of them would be useful. The photographer, a melancholy little man who had rejected Julian's offer of a jaunty feathered hat, scowled; he hated working with children – you never knew what faces the little blighters were going to make at the last moment and you didn't find out until their smirks and grimaces emerged from the developing fluid.

Anne wore a demure gown with puffy sleeves and a close fitting white cotton bonnet. She was rather hot, as she had kept her own blouse underneath to avoid contact with the costume. You never knew who had been the last person to wear something like that, or whether it had been properly laundered.

"*What a gay day.*" Jonny looked droopier than usual as he pulled up his tights again. Anne had chosen for him a costume designed for a beefier child.

"Oh, I think I like dressing up," decided Julie, holding her long skirts to her sides. She smiled at the photographer and he clicked thankfully.

"Come along, Jonny. It's fun having our own castle," said Anne. "You don't get chances like this very often."

"*What do you think of the show so far? Rubbish!*"

"What's that dear? Oh, here's Dick, or *Sir* Dick." Anne made a mock curtsey to her brother.

"My Lady Anne," Dick responded, bowing as low as his costume allowed and making a flourish with his arm. "My Lady Julie!" He repeated the gesture, making Julie giggle, and was going to do so again with her sibling, but Jonny had wandered off. With an effort Anne stopped herself following him. She had, several times, recalled the image of her son laughing and waving his hands around the scrappy little bonfire earlier, and decided to try letting Jonny find his feet a bit tonight. She was making a good effort.

"Pretty cool, eh?" asked Dick, turning around to show the

full effect of his outfit. The resemblance was to Henry VIII in his later years. He had chosen it with Jo in the games room, and they had both laughed at its absurdities. Jo had looked very sprightly in her costume, but had disappeared behind the scenes to supervise the catering. Julian still hadn't a clue who she was, but Anne had squeezed her arm by the tapestry and said some warm words, which Jo had quite appreciated.

The sounds of vaguely medieval strings and somewhat unlikely female singers wafted through the hall from the speakers discreetly hidden under the dais and within the suits of armour, and whenever a new guest arrived Julian intended that they would play a fanfare, though this was proving a little challenging technically. He had a twin deck cassette player wired up for the purpose, but the pause button was dodgy. Quentin managed to get more than half of a trumpet solo as he entered the Hall, and was playing up to his role, wearing a huge fur trimmed coat on his back and Yu Na on his arm. Julian looked again at Bianca with slight regret. Her costume went all the way up to a high neckline – such a waste. Bianca saw him, and gave him a cool wink. As Quentin was here Fanny, of course, couldn't be. Their mutual animosity would wreck the whole evening, and couldn't be risked. Julian had found himself in a bit of a quandary when it came to Quentin and Fanny. There was a lot of potential for publicity with both of them. On balance, Quentin was likely to attract a wider demographic including boys and fathers. Fanny had become (he pondered the word) *unreliable*. Still, once Kirrin Cottage had become part of the Experience there would be a role for her, too.

Julian looked around the room and allowed himself a few deep breaths. So. Everyone was here except George. Would she come? Would she stay? And for one evening set aside her penchant for making off with boats? Hugh had reported that George couldn't been found anywhere, and nobody had seen her since she had handed over the keys to the launch more than two hours ago. He would have to get her sorted out.

Back in Kirrin Cottage the panel in the study yielded without that much difficulty. George was strong, despite her aching muscles, and Fanny excited. In the event, Fanny was surprisingly agile, and Gary was the least keen, but followed along with a little coaxing. Timmy was never so reluctant. Behind the panel, there was nothing too steep in the way of the steps leading downwards, and the three figures moved cautiously but largely unimpeded. The paths were in better order than George had expected, and the distance shorter than it had seemed in the past. She had a powerful torch with her, which she had found in the cottage.

"Come on, Mother, hold onto me," she whispered. Fanny seemed invigorated, and chatted excitedly, though rather incoherently. George paused for a minute at an awkward heap of rocks, and the muted sound of the sea booming overhead gave her a surge of adrenaline. She half lifted her mother over the rubble.

"Alright, Mother, over you go. Now you know what we're doing, don't you? We're gate-crashing Julian's stupid banquet and showing Father who's boss. Your job is to be as angry as you like, and tell everyone there what a complete bastard he has been. Tell him that this place is *mine*, or rather yours and mine, and I want it back. Got it?"

"Got it, dear," replied her mother, a little vaguely.

As she realised that they were approaching the dungeons, George's spirits rose further – this was going to be fun. Even

Gary managed a wag of his tail, and stopped to scratch at one of the doors in quite an animated fashion. George tugged him on. There was the door they needed. George's biggest fear was that it might be locked against them, but thankfully it could be opened from their side, and the three of them negotiated their way slowly out of the trapdoor in the courtyard, into the air. It was getting dark, but the evening was still warm. George took a moment to look out to sea, to the old wreck gleaming with some early stars behind it, and a few lights of Kirrin twinkling on the mainland. She helped her mother across the courtyard and into the castle by the side door. This place was worth fighting for.

Once inside, George was unsure of the best way to make an entrance. They went through into a smallish corridor, George holding a rather eager Fanny back. The kitchen door swung open beside them and a waitress, pushing her way through with her bottom first, collided with them both, deftly righting her tray of chicken drumsticks and spinning round as she did so. Fanny beamed suddenly.

"Goodness, George dear, isn't it lovely that little Jo is here to help you all again. Such a brave little scrap! A little Raggle-Taggle Gypsy-O!" George stared at the waitress.

"Jo? Surely…?"

"Well, so you've noticed at last! I didn't think I'd changed *that* much. *You* haven't, not except that you need a good pair of glasses!" Her voice was feisty, and stirred up George's blood, the way it always had in one way or another.

"Jo! Bloody hell!" Jo looked amused, and after an awkward hug and a few minutes of explanation about the launch and their plans, she had provided the pair with a good goblet of mead each and ushered George and Fanny past the Great Hall and into the games room, where she showed them the racks of clothes.

"Here you are. Keep clear of the corsets," she said, grimacing at her own. "There's a few bits and pieces there you might not object to, George Kirrin."

There was more giggling and shushing as George and Fanny surveyed the choices on offer among the costumes, which were rather jumbled after the others had had their pick. Gary's burrowing around added to the chaos, but after sashaying about holding up some splendid gowns for her mother, and toying briefly with a nun's habit, George settled on an acceptably androgynous pageboy's outfit for herself, and a rather elegant and dignified dress for her mother. The two of them got togged up, George helping her mother with the lacing and priming her with a few choice lines about equality and power to declaim at Quentin and Julian. They were going to do this in style.

Julian smiled in relief as George strode in, and, as a celebrated guest, the assistant found the tape with the fanfare to announce her, getting about three-quarters of the trumpet solo out before pressing the off switch with a clunk. But George was not alone. Julian saw with concern the swaying figure of Fanny Kirrin with her head held high in a black gown, long train and tall hat. George was turning and bowing to her, and making her the centre of attention. Gary followed behind them all, trailing a rag from his mouth which Julian hoped wasn't one of the more expensive fabrics. George was beginning to sing, rather gruffly and tunelessly.

"We shall overco-o-ome. We shall overco-o-ome…" Fanny started to join in, as George had instructed, with a thin vibrato voice in an entirely different key waving her arms to invite the others to join her.

Quentin turned his attention from Yu Na and spoke harshly to Julian.

"What are you playing at? Nobody told me she was coming. Get her out of here. You know what will happen." Julian shot a sideways look to the photographer.

"Nobody told me, either," he hissed. Fanny beamed seraphically and began wafting about like one of those almost-pensioned-off aged prima ballerinas, acting out their last years onstage as Juliet's mother, showing occasional glimpses of grace and beauty. She was enjoying herself immensely.

"We shall overco-o-ome. We shall…George, what about 'Smoke Gets in Your Eyes'? That's a lovely one."

Julian eyed Fanny furiously, but quickly changed his look to one of familial affection. A scene now would be disastrous.

"Aunt Fanny! How wonderful that you could come to our gathering! Do let me find you somewhere comfortable to sit." He had to contain these rogue females. Fanny airily waved away the offer and posed a few times for the camera, pleased after so many years to be the centre of attention. She moved on to 'Second Hand Rose', with no sense of irony whatsoever.

George moved away, furious. This wasn't disruptive, it was feeble. She'd had in mind something more like the invasion of the Miss World contest, loud and strong. But she hadn't got any supporters. She was stuck with her mother, who was behaving like Lady Bountiful and unlikely to provoke anything but indulgent smiles. It was an anti-climax and an embarrassment, and things would get worse if she didn't keep her mother away from the mead.

Fanny and her daughter began a sort of side stepping duet around the jugs of mead on the table. Neither would explicitly allow the other to see that they knew what was going on. As the minutes went on Fanny became more vigorous, more insistent, until her side steps started to make her tall hat wobble.

Julian came to a decision. He walked over for a quick con-sultation with Bianca. The lights came up to full power, bathing the hall in sudden light. He walked up to the dais in front of the finest seat and raised his arms.

"Welcome, nobles, ladies, esquires. Welcome family and friends. Welcome to this court in the Great Hall of Kirrin Cas-tle. May this be the first of many happy evenings with Kirrin Enterprises! Now, please all take your seats and let the feasting commence!"

As *Carmina Burana* burst forth, drowning Fanny's fading warbles, the wenches helped the guests to their places in high backed armchairs. George decided to play along and keep her powder dry until the right moment, and clenched her mouth tight shut. Julian, meanwhile, had left the dais and was parading around the family table in full lordly fashion. He stopped by Anne.

"Anne! I do hope you are enjoying all this wonderful food. Do you remember all that cold tongue rubbish we used to eat?"

"Oh dear, yes! I suppose it was rather dreadful, some of it," said Anne. "I mean, one never quite knew what went into all that potted meat we had in our sandwiches. We always eat home-cooked food."

"No, we don't, Mummy. We went to McDonald's on the way here," pointed out Julie, smirking slightly. Anne blushed, but then smiled.

"We did, didn't we! Well anyway, all those salads were terribly good for us, and the fresh fruit. We used to eat it straight from the garden. I mean, Timmy could have…you know…in the vegetable plot. But we were all fine, weren't we? Perhaps we could try some sausages on your next camp fire." She gave Julie a squeeze. "Oh, is that more mead? Yes, please, it's really refreshing! It's a honey drink, isn't it? Probably really healthy! I feel sort of aglow – all over!"

Everyone roared with laughter, even George, and Anne beamed round the table. Jonny beamed, too.

"Tell 'em about the honey, Mummy!"

What could have been a disaster was, in the end, hugely enjoyed by everyone. George forgot herself. They all forgot themselves. They played their characters, laughed, and quaffed, and quaffed again. Anne, delighted with her new taste for the nutritious honey drink, stopped worrying about whether the twins were eating anything other than chips, and prompted by Julie got up to dance, performing a startling and slightly *Pan's People* interpretation of the stately music.

Julian toasted Bianca, Quentin toasted Yu Na, and Hugh and Radclyffe toasted each other. George even stopped worrying about her mother's quaffing and quaffed herself. Julian was so relieved he clapped her on the back and said something about consulting her to set up ethical supply chains and access to the island for more unfortunate souls than themselves. He then toasted George, raising his goblet and pressing it against hers – *the spirit of the island!* The others joined in – *to George – the spirit of Kirrin Island!* The camera clicked, Anne hiccupped loudly, and Aunt Fanny beamed at them all from her semi-supine position on a huge carved chair full of nylon velvet cushions.

Something happened to George at that moment. She felt a strange letting go – a sort of unfurrowing. Her family *liked* her, liked her even after her efforts to ruin the evening. She liked them, too, just a bit. Oh, there was all sorts of rubbish going on, but fundamentally there was some sort of hope for them all. Look at them!

Dick, who had popped out to the kitchen for a few stolen kisses with Jo, came back with her on his arm like a cat with two tails. The others squashed up, and Jo sat between them and grinned at her old enemy George, while Aunt Fanny started to snore contentedly. Gary pushed in and out between the legs under the table picking up the tastiest morsels. The old hall rang to sound of happy laughter. Julian, too, had a warm *I think we are going to pull this off* feeling. He felt the twitch in his eye melt away.

Eventually, when the twins were dozing on a pile of cloaks, and the staff had finished off the dregs of mead, Julian stood slightly unsteadily on his dais again with Bianca and tapped his glass with a spoon.

"All I can do now is raise a glass to Kirrins – family, island and castle! And to friends!" He waved his glass in Jo's direction. "Um…God bless us every one! That is…er…"

Jonny stirred.

"*Time for bed, said Zebedee,*" he said, drowsily, and everyone laughed again.

They left the castle and tottered down the little hill in the dark, their way lit by flaming torches. Hugh, still sober, navigated carefully between the twinkling buoys in the big launch, brought them safely to the quayside, and helped them ashore. Radclyffe escorted his grandmother home, and everyone fell into their beds exhausted and happy.

24

A Horrid Surprise!

Waking up in the morning with a hangover is not the best start to anyone's day and Julian rarely found himself in such an annoying position. Although used to rising early, he preferred a gentle awakening: black coffee and a leisurely cigarette. He was most certainly *not* used to a party of large men in uniform bursting into his bedroom before the sun was up and shouting at him. He sat up in bed, and stared at the bulky man advancing towards him.

"Mr. Julian Kirrin?"

"Yes. What is going on?" He felt vulnerable, sitting there in his silk pyjamas. It was an unaccustomed feeling.

"Mr. Kirrin, I am a Police Officer and I have a warrant to search these premises."

This was obviously a ridiculous mistake. Julian wondered if the local constabulary had got the wrong end of some stick, but the policeman didn't sound local. He held on to his blankets.

"What the hell is going on?" Julian's normally well-modulated tones betrayed a sense of growing discomfort which less controlled individuals might have called panic. "Why are you in *my* room?"

"I will ask the questions, Mr. Kirrin," responded the policeman brusquely as the officers spread around the room.

"Is this your suit, sir?" asked one, lifting a jacket from the trouser press.

"Yes, of course," snapped Julian. "I'm not in the habit of wearing anyone else's clothes."

"And is this yours?" The policeman removed a small silver pill box from the pocket.

"Well, er, it depends," said Julian. He tried to remain cool, but his head was starting to spin. Damn. The policeman opened the lid and sniffed the contents.

"And will you tell me what this is, sir?" asked the policeman, walking closer and holding out the open box.

"What? I don't know. How should I know? What do you mean?" Julian's face was turning the same colour as the white substance inside. Damn, again.

"Mr. Julian Kirrin," said the burly Sergeant in charge, "I have reason to believe this substance is a controlled drug and I am arresting you. You do not have to say anything, but anything you do say may be taken down and given in evidence against you."

Damn, damn, damn. It was such a tiny bit. Really small. He didn't even use it, really. Not in the way most of his city-slicker associates did. It was there just in case his twitchy eye got out of control. If this had been the city...

"You must be off your head!" growled Julian under his breath, but, brain whirling, he quickly changed his strategy and forced a slightly tight smile. This required charm not threats. "OK, but this really isn't anything at all. I'm sure we can reach an agreement about this business, as gentlemen, men of the world and so forth. Now how about..."

"Cuff him, lads," ordered the Sergeant. The two hefty policemen leapt on Julian and pinned him to the floor, quite unnecessarily, his face pressed into the heavy pile of the rug. Damn wasn't the word.

*

176

Anne's awakening was slightly less startling, at least initially. After the jolly events of the night before, and all that lovely honey drink, she had not prepared herself for bed with quite her usual care. That thought went through her mind when the door opened and she heard someone walk into the room.

"It must be one of the children with tea. How kind," she decided. Her eyes weren't quite ready to open yet, though. The light through the crack in the curtains would be a little jarring at present. Tea, though, was the cup that cheers.

"Hello, darling. How lovely! It's just what I need, with this silly headache." Her voice was loving, half covered by the eiderdown.

"I am not your darling, madam, I am WPC Hendy." The announcement was loud and woke Anne up in a flash. She sat up to face a stern looking woman at the side of her bed, and she wasn't carrying the cup that cheers.

"Oh, my goodness! What's happening? Are the children alright?"

"Yes, Madam, perfectly alright. Social Services will be informed, if necessary. It is the usual procedure."

"What do you mean? Is there anything I can do? I am a trained counsellor, you know?" Anne started to get out of bed, still confused, but eager to help.

"No thank you, madam. Just stay where you are please, while we search your room."

"Er, of course." She sat back down. "Are you looking for anything in particular? Is something missing from the pub? Do let me know if I can help?" Anne, helpful as ever, leaned forward and reached her dressing gown from the bottom of the bed. How untidy, she thought. I must have been very tired.

"Let me help you, madam," said the WPC, putting one hand into the pocket and picking up Anne's handbag with the other. "So, everything here is yours, is it?"

"Yes, officer, certainly."

"And there is nothing here that you shouldn't have?"

How strange. Anne thought hard. It wasn't theft to have put those little soaps from the bathroom in her bag, was it? Just in case she needed to wash her hands properly while she was out?

"No, I don't think so."

"Thank you, madam, my colleagues will just satisfy ourselves that there is nothing amiss."

Anne sat up straighter in bed, the covers pulled up round her knees, and watched in confusion as the two women in overalls went methodically round the room opening and examining everything. One went into the bathroom.

It was beginning to seem as if they had finished when the policewoman emerged from the bathroom with a small Tupperware container in her gloved hand. She showed it to the one in charge, who prised the lid off, peered at the contents, sniffed and nodded.

"Then this is yours too, is it?" she asked, politely.

"Yes, of course. I mean, it must be! I mean…oh heavens," said Anne. She thought it was, but then again, she had so many…

The policewoman looked at her seriously. "Madam, you are under arrest on suspicion of possession of a controlled substance. I must tell you that you do not have to say anything but anything you do say will be taken down and may be used in evidence."

Anne gasped and crumpled back on the pillows – this was terrible. What would she say to the children? And Rupert?

For Dick the humiliation was even greater. It wasn't just that he was a policeman, though that was bad enough, but there were even more important things now – things that had gone so well the previous night. Full of drink and good cheer he had fallen asleep with happy thoughts about his future: Nigel would bust the drugs ring operating around Kirrin, Dick would be recognised as the alert and sharp-witted instigator of the success, and there would be an end to his unsatisfactory mundane life. Promotion in the Force would follow, and, best of all, the chance of a real future with Jo. Optimistic *and* realistic, for a change, he had thought. The sound of the door being opened with a key registered only vaguely, and the dark figure coming into his room only a little more clearly.

"Good morning, sir. I am PC Nutbeam. Just you stay where you are."

"Oh, breakfast – wonderful," he mumbled from under the covers. "Over there – on the table." He gestured with his arm. Worried about whether he should be offering a tip for this unexpected room service he lifted the covers a little. "Look in there."

"Thank you, sir," replied the surprised policeman, holding Dick's canvas bag. "Is this yours, Sir?"

"Yes, look inside."

"Certainly, sir." The policeman held out what looked like a decent sized wrap of cannabis "And this?" he enquired.

Dick tried to understand what was going on, but his wits were not at their sharpest. He didn't possess cannabis. He didn't even smoke. Surely this wasn't what was supposed to be happening?

"I'm sorry to say, sir, that I shall have to ask you to accompany me to the station. I think you know the rest. If you would like to put some clothes on. We'll have to use these, of course, just for the look of the thing." The policeman started to unlock his handcuffs. Was that a wink in Dick's direction?

"Er, of course, anything you say." Dick still felt slightly puzzled, but he was used to obeying authority. PC Nutbeam's face contorted into another wink. Dick thought for a moment, and with a sigh of relief winked back. Of course! This was part of his cover, part of his protection from the revenge of the gang. Perfect!

Things were not going so quietly in George's room.

"Fascist!" she yelled.

"I'm sorry, Madam, but that won't help matters," said the policewoman, not entirely apologetically. She was young, fresh-faced and ambitious. This was exciting stuff.

"Get her, Gary! Get her!" urged George, trying to rouse the animal by kicking him from underneath the covers.

"Don't involve your dog, Madam," warned the policewoman, who, seeing that Gary was disinclined to leap into action on behalf of his owner, remained calm, and even pleasant. She had been trying to iron out her Birmingham twang in recent weeks, but it always got the better of her at exciting times.

"You can't arrest me! I've got rights, and I know them." George reached for her dungarees in a fury.

"Just stay where you are, madam." The policewoman swept the dungarees off the floor and felt inside the big pocket on the bib. She pulled out a 'These Are Your Rights' card, which George carried with her everywhere. She, too, had read that useful manual *Signs of Crime*. She knew cards such as these were carried by agitators, Angry Brigade inadequates, homosexuals and amateur criminals who were likely to make false complaints. She knew to be circumspect with intellectual malcontents who could be bitchy and small-minded. It was all in the book.

"Don't worry, madam, I'm just doing my duty," she said

calmly. "Everything will be done by the book, and we'll be very fair. If you've done nothing wrong, you have nothing to fear."

Gary, meanwhile, had roused himself, and having rolled off the bed and yawned was lumbering across the room towards the sleek police dog which was sniffing urgently at George's rucksack. The dogs faced each other and bared their teeth, but kept a few feet apart.

The policewoman reached into the canvas, rummaging among the paperback books and dog biscuits, and pulled out a rectangular tin with a distinctive leaf on the lid. George leapt to her feet on the bed.

"Fascist!" She was almost jumping up and down on the mattress in her outrage.

"Now, madam, calm down. You can explain everything down at the station," said the WPC.

"I'm not going anywhere! Get me a lawyer! Get me the NCCL! You're setting me up!" George slumped down on to the bed, sullenly folding her arms.

"I'm sorry, Madam but the National Council for Civil Liberties isn't available at 5am." Walking to the door and leaning into the corridor, her young heart thrilling at the command she was about to utter, she called "Snatch Squad, please." Immediately two substantial policewomen rushed into the room, and soon George's cries could be heard echoing down the corridor.

25

The News Gets Round

Not until it pulled up outside The Kirrin Arms did Bianca remember Julian's insistence that they charter a luxury coach for some of Fleet Street's more amenable travel writers. His idea was a preview release of The Kirrin Island Experience. The press pack envelopes had been prepared but she left them in the box in the pub office for now. First, she would need to employ all her charms placating the grumpy gentlemen of the press who had been told to expect a charming and heart-warming story of family enterprise and holiday delights worthy of being dragged to the sticks at the weekend for.

This was a situation to be managed on the hoof – keeping them inside would minimise the chance of them finding out just why the Kirrins were not there to meet them. Having persuaded Jo to open the bar early, Bianca ushered the travel hacks in. Free drinks would keep them quiet for a while and everything would be resolved. Julian would be back with the others by lunchtime.

Joan was all of a dither, as she put it to Fred Pitts in the shop that morning. The little place was humming with the good folk of Kirrin. The subject, of course, was the arrest of four members of the best known local family. Everyone would be part of the drama by vague association and spurious inside knowledge.

The tongues were busy. Joan glared at them. The family had been in the papers when they had discovered all that gold in the tunnels, and again when they'd foiled no end of criminals. Proud of them all, she had been.

"This don't seem right to me. Half-a-crown's one thing, especially when you're a kiddie and might of got a bit mixed up, now I think about it, but I'd *never* have thought...*never*..." And she didn't think it now, whatever the rest of them were saying. Those children were decent souls.

"Look!" exclaimed an excited customer. "There's a big chara-banc coming in. It's full of men!" She jerked her child away from a display of Fray Bentos with a twitch of the toddler reins and hurried outside to see what was going on.

26

The Cells are Not Very Nice

It wasn't exactly the reunion that Julian had planned. They *were* all together but they were also all locked up. The journey had begun badly, crammed in the back of the police van and bumped along the potholes. At the County Police Headquarters they had been led down corridors with peeling paint and broken light fittings to separate cells where they had been left behind noisily locked doors to contemplate their fates, whatever they might be.

Dick was the least uncomfortable – he knew what this was about, and he didn't expect to be there long. He just wished he had had a chance to let the others know that it was all a cover, and they would be OK, but they hadn't been allowed to speak to each other. Julian insisted on having his solicitor in London called and kept asking whether he had arrived. George decided that embracing her detention would really help her understand what it was like to be oppressed. Anne sat on the horrible bed trying not to whimper and worrying about the children.

The first hour was bearable. It would all be sorted out and they would be gone soon. As the morning wore on, though, each of them began to feel growing doubts. Nothing was happening.

Upstairs, however, there was a lot going on – men coming and going, talking into radios and having whispered conversation on the telephone. At eleven, the Drug Squad arrived from

London wearing jeans, sweatshirts and long hair which they supposed made them look less like policemen. The local police in their uniforms resented their constant demands for office space, private telephones and access to the canteen.

"This is it – the big one," insisted a bearded individual whose long hair and colourful shirt particularly offended the Sergeant. "We've had a hot tip-off."

The trouble was, they weren't getting very far. They had searched every nook and cranny of the hotel, and then the cars. Next, they brought in the sniffer dogs. Still nothing. One of the fisherman took them over to Kirrin Island, where they combed the castle – nothing there either. They did find the entrance to the dungeon and the tunnels leading away from it, though none of them fancied disappearing into the darkness. Orders on this were confusing, as the radio communications back to the mainland were crackly and intermittent.

"A dungeon? What, an actual dungeon? Yes, of course I want you to go down – where do you think anyone would hide things – in a dungeon! Of course it's bloody dark. Take the dogs."

At lunchtime Julian's solicitor arrived from London, pinstriped and pompous, and one by one the cousins were interviewed. On his solicitor's advice Julian, furious but cool, made no comment. George had read her NCCL These are Your Rights card and refused to speak. Anne explained at length that she didn't know *anything* about drugs, while using up a whole box of tissues.

Dick's interview was the most awkward. The officers of the law, like Dick, knew the interview was a show version for the record. This was reassuring at first – Nigel must have straightened things out with the Squad – but it was followed by a much longer unofficial discussion about what Dick actually knew, which turned out to be next to nothing. He was taken back to his cell with the distinct impression this wasn't going well. What would Jo think of him now?

27

Down in the Tunnels Again

Things were starting to look up for the police on Kirrin Island. At about 2.30 one of the sniffer dogs, a feisty little terrier, yelped hard, got excited and disappeared down one of the tunnels. This was it – they had found something now.

The dog scrabbled noisily at a large locked door, and the men set to with a collective heave of the shoulders. The door gave way, and they tumbled through. Minutes later they emerged with no drugs, no hostage and no contraband. Instead they carried a small dog which they had found wagging its tail, surrounded by boxes. These, though, were full of nothing more incriminating than tins of Chum. They tried a few cans – opening them with penknives, but there wasn't anything inside which the sniffer dog wasn't eager to eat. The reports, when they came through, were dispiriting to the waiting police.

"A dog? Bloody dog food? Bugger health and safety," barked the head of the Drugs Squad to his tired and grumbling crew. "The radios are working again, so get back down those tunnels. There's miles of them."

The underground passages were darker and more confusing the further under the sea they went, twisting and branching left and right. Concerned about getting lost they tried letting out a roll of string but it wasn't long enough. Finally, they came to a halt – a large metal door blocked their way.

"You found what?" the head of the Drug Squad shouted into his radio. "Iron doors? Of course I want you to find out what's on the other side. Blow the bloody doors off if you have to!"

28

The Press Get Annoyed

Hours passed, and Julian wasn't back. After a few drinks, the press men became excitable and irritated, despite her best efforts. Bianca, assisted by Jo, placated them as best she could. No, Jo told them, as they began peering through the windows, she didn't know why there were two policemen who seemed to be guarding the end of the quay. No, she didn't know why the fishermen were standing about by their boats and hadn't gone out on such a lovely day. No, she didn't think they would take anyone for a trip over to that island with the little castle that looked so inviting. As the excuses became thinner and less convincing blood alcohol levels rose and demands became louder and less polite.

"Look, darlings," one of them was saying, "we've been told there's a story, and if we don't get it we're all getting back on that coach to London and the only story we're going to write is that nothing happens in this little dump and the beer's been watered down." Bianca smiled, with some effort, but before she could think of anything to say a shadow fell on the bar. A huge army truck chugged past the window onto the quayside. Another followed, and another, which stopped outside, leaving the bar in semi-darkness. Scenting a story, the newshounds put down their pints and, fumbling for their notebooks and cameras, rushed towards the door.

They didn't get far – two soldiers with rifles had set up station at the main exit, and two more began putting up a canvas screen across the entrance to the quay. This was a story, for sure, but what story? Some kind kind of emergency? A film? Even Saatchi & Saatchi didn't have the resources to pull a publicity stunt this big. The hubbub stopped when a serious looking man in uniform came into the bar and raised a gloved hand for silence. Tenterhooks were fully employed as the pens quivered.

"Gentlemen," he said, "my name is Brigadier Lethbridge-Stewart. We are dealing with an incident, the nature of which I cannot disclose. I apologise that we must restrict your movements, but for your own safety you will not be allowed to leave this building until further notice. There will be no use of the telephone," he raised his hand again, "and no questions."

He turned his back and was gone.

29

What is Going On?

Hours passed. The assembled writers were used to being wined and dined while enjoying the sun at Mediterranean resorts. While they might frequent *El Vino's* the pleasures of a seaside village pub in the daytime were wearing thinner than a punk rocker's bin bag. Cheated of a scoop, they returned to the consolation of the bar. A couple of the more enterprising found their way up the back stairs to a window from where they could see trucks being unloaded and tents set up on the quay, with tantalising glimpses of men in white suits inside them. Inflatable boats were seen disappearing around the far side of the island. Were those men in uniform abseiling down the cliffs?

Then soldiers had entered their room, escorted the gentlemen down the stairs, taken all the film out of their cameras and locked everyone in the bar. The more imaginative hacks immediately started writing opinion pieces and interviewing each other about their experience of this unprecedented event. At least that would give some copy to file when they got back or could get to a telephone. *Quiet village shaken by Army invasion. Alien terror on our shores! Was I caught up in a rehearsal for a military coup?*

30

Back in the Cells

Julian's solicitor began to enjoy himself, and stopped pretending to hide his contempt for the provincial constabulary.

"So, Inspector, what have you got against my clients? An insignificant bit of 'personal' that any competent bobby on the street in London would find every day, and give a caution for. If this was the Glastonbury Festival you wouldn't even have bothered. Look at the waste of resources! You're going to be a laughing stock. The only people in trouble here are you and your friends in the Drug Squad, and your colleague from the Met. I can see the headlines now – *Drug Squad speed down A303 to arrest innocent Met officer and family.* Or are you going to charge him with having a dog without a licence? Not exactly the crime of the century. Look, we'll do a deal. I'm sure I've got thirty-seven pence on me – shall I just buy him one and you can call the whole thing off?"

They had to agree that if nothing more turned up by seven in the evening they would let the Kirrins go.

Seven o'clock came and went and nothing more had been found. The cell doors of Dorset HQ were opened and the prisoners brought out to sit round a big table and be reunited with their belongings.

"I'm suing," said Julian as he did up his wristwatch. "As soon as I get out of here, I'm suing."

"Me too," fumed George, "and the NCCL is going to know about it."

Anne's relief was the greatest. All she wanted to do was get out of the horrid place, find the children and have a wash. Julian reached out and held his sister's hand.

Dick was silent. This wasn't how it was supposed to be. He'd been so sure that something was going on. He couldn't explain the dog either, unless there had been some mix up over Gary. He couldn't look the others in the eye. Glum was the word. A commotion in the corridor outside – quick footsteps and raised voices – made him raise his eyes hopefully.

"Oh no," thought Julian. "The hell-hounds of the press have arrived." But they hadn't. The door almost left its hinges as the head of the Drug Squad burst in, breathless and ashen-faced.

"You lot, don't move. You're going nowhere. We've found something. We've found lots of things. I'm arresting you all under the Terrorism Act."

31

Nothing to Report

The Brigadier reappeared, and raised his hand for silence.

"Gentlemen, I again thank you for your patience. I still cannot tell you anything, and these," he started handing round bits of paper, "are D Notices issued under the Official Secrets Act which prohibit any reporting of anything you may have seen today. If you will follow me, your coach will now return you to London where your editors will also have been served with D Notices. I do not expect to read anything in the papers over my breakfast tomorrow."

32

A Letter from Anne

Holloway Women's Prison, Remand Wing

Darling Julie and Jonny,

Two whole days have gone by since the silly mix-up. You must not worry about Mummy *at all*. My little room here is quite snug, with a bed and table, and a sink, and a shelf for my toothbrush and photographs of you two. I do hope you are both cleaning your teeth properly.

I have talked to Daddy about all sorts of things to tell Mrs. Finniston so she can keep everything the way we like it, and he says that he feels so bad about not being at home to help you with your prep, he might ask his secretary, Miss Perkins, to come and stay with you all for a day or two, to make things easier. That sounds like an awfully good idea. I believe she is very kind and generous.

Darlings, Mummy has explained about what a dreadful misunderstanding all of this is. You know that I haven't done anything wrong *at all*. I am sure all the clever lawyers will soon find out all about what really happened, and then I can come home to you all again. When I do, we will have some really jolly times together, I promise. I think it would be lovely to have another go at lighting a fire, don't you? I haven't forgotten about the marshmallows, either. If Daddy is too busy we can leave him to get on with his work.

I must go now, my darlings. The bell has rung, which is just like school, isn't it! Please write to Mummy just as soon as you can, and tell me all your news. Oh dear, there is a lot of hammering on the door. Now if we had little doorbells it would feel so much cosier.

With lots of love,
Mummy.

33

George is Determined

Holloway Women's Prison, Remand Wing

OK, Radclyffe, I'd better tell you a few things. First, I will get out of this dump soon. I am innocent.

Next thing is, make sure you take Gary with you if you go out at night. And eat some proper food, OK? There must be stuff at the Barbican flat. I suppose Hugh sorts it out. Has Gary wrecked Julian's furniture yet?

I want to talk to you about what we do when I get out of here. You liked it at Kirrin, didn't you? I'm not exactly Anne, but I did actually see you getting interested in stuff – boats and so on. You are quite a lot like me in that. We'll talk, OK?

Anne is just something else. She's on a kind of mission to turn this place into The Little House on the Prairie or something. I saw her trying to turn toilet paper into napkins yesterday. God help her cellmate! She is being kind, though, when she's not fretting about the twins. Really kind.

Are they alright? Are you alright? Actually, I miss you.
Ma.

34

Julian Learns about Prison

Wandsworth Prison, Remand Wing

My dear Hugh,

I apologise about the pencil – apparently a fountain pen is too dangerous.

The police claims about all the things found in the tunnels are ridiculous. I hope we can keep that out of the papers, though they do say any publicity is good. If it falls to me to start a fight to cut out the cancer of bent and twisted journalism in our country with the simple sword of truth and the trusty shield of British fair play, so be it. I am ready for the fight.

I can't say anything about the people or conditions here – I'm sure the censor will be reading this. Like the city, you need to get to know the right people, and I'm making connections. Perhaps also gaining a little insight into the lives of these people.

I trust you and Bianca to keep business under control until this is all sorted out. I'll be fine. If you can, do visit Anne, or take her twins out for a treat, or something.

I don't know how long this will last – but *nil carborundum iillegitimi*.

Your loving father.

35

A Letter to Jo

Stamped HM Prison Wandsworth – held back by censor

My dear, dear Jo,

I know this looks bad, but it's all a misunderstanding. All I can think about is you and getting out of here and getting back to you. That is, if you will have me. I won't be surprised if you won't.

I must be a stupid sort of a person to have landed in this mess. I thought I knew something, but it was not what I thought. I only wanted to do the right thing and I think I've done the wrong thing, and now I've made things awful for all of us.

I expected to get arrested, as part of my cover, but my mate Nigel, who I told about the Operation T Telex thingie, and the lights, hasn't come to see me yet, so I don't know what is going on. It doesn't tell you about this in *Signs of Crime* and I'm confused.

I didn't expect them to arrest Anne, and Julian and George, but when we were being taken away in the boat I thought that must be cover for them, too. But they haven't let them go either, and now they are asking me about explosives and nerve gas and toxic waste and I know NOTHING about that. There are rumours that we might all get moved to Cat A because we might be a threat to national security. Us? National security? I don't get it.

The food here isn't as good as your ham sandwiches, but I'm going to start eating some stuff like carrots and doing some press-ups. I'm sharing with a body builder called Charles. He tells me that as long I don't annoy him I'll be OK. I don't annoy him.

I really hope things aren't bad for you. Thank God you weren't arrested, too. I'd do anything to be out of here and with you again.

Ever, ever yours,

Dick XXXX

36

An Awkward Meeting in Whitehall

Quentin Kirrin passed like a whirlwind through the normally sedate corridors of Whitehall, despite the walking stick. Once his old connections had got him through the doors he had passed rapidly up the hierarchy, a hot potato everyone wanted to pass on, with a whiff of ticking time bomb about his old jacket. As this irresistible force was passed from office to office the furnishings became plusher and the waits became longer. He had reached the pinnacle of the civil service but his temper was no better and his patience no greater. He tapped his stick against the polished parquet floor.

"The Cabinet Secretary will see you shortly," said the woman behind the mahogany desk for the fifth time, "but he cannot be interrupted." She lowered her voice. "He is engaged with the Prime Minister."

"Even better," said Quentin, getting up and striding towards the door. His cane pointed ahead. "The Prime Minister is a chemist – she will understand."

"No, Professor Kirrin," she cried, stepping across in front of him. "Please be seated – you will be seen."

This was a half-truth – the Cabinet Secretary was not with the Prime Minister, he was scratching his head over a big pile of papers that had arrived on his desk. Over the previous two days messages had been making their way upwards, memos had been hurriedly composed, and vans had been sent to retrieve files that were never meant to be found again. Retired senior civil servants had been found and interrupted in the middle of games of bridge. Generals who had gone to earth had been harassed in their clubs by polite young men from departments that did not exist.

So now Sir Robert Armstrong had before him one quite thin file, on the events at Kirrin, and several very thick ones which related to the career of Professor Quentin Kirrin, FRS, RIC, FREng. The thin one was a problem, certainly, but it was the thick ones that concerned him most. He wished he had not read them, he did not want anyone else to read them, and he wanted them all to go away. But this had to be done and the old bugger seen. Sighing, he flicked a switch on the console on his desk.

"Please ask Professor Kirrin to come in."

Quentin Kirrin had never had much respect for stuffed shirts and pen pushers and nobody he had met in the past forty-eight hours had changed his opinion.

"Professor Kirrin, I am…"

"I know who you are and you know who I am," he fired back, ignoring the proffered handshake. "How much have they told you?"

"I have been made aware that four people have been arrested under the Terrorism Act on what appears to be cogent evidence and under proper procedures. The circumstances may cause some embarrassment. A D Notice has been issued." The very civil servant maintained his calm. The less civil professor was almost nonchalant.

"Your plodding policemen have been galumphing through my old laboratories on Kirrin Island – the laboratories that you insisted had been locked up securely and which *your* lot said could not be entered again by anybody without the deepest level of authorisation. Operation Hades was the name of this arrangement – long term storage of hazardous waste deep underground. Nobody has died – yet. Your arrangements were shoddy, it seems." Sir Robert blenched, but the old scientist continued. "Thankfully, when the local plods found the stuff behind a pretty amateur metal door they had the sense to call in the Army, and there are still some people at Porton Down who can read labels. When I stopped my work for the government I asked the MoD to take every last toxic substance to Porton Down or to bury them with the waste from Sellafield, and you told me they would remain only until such time as these arrangements could be made. But dearie, dearie me, you haven't done it. I *said* this would happen."

"I am aware of that and appropriate measures are being take to secure the site." Sir Robert's calm was getting more difficult to maintain.

"How much have they actually told you?" Quentin challenged. "I have, at the request of her Majesty's Government, experimented with many compounds; anthrax, botulinum and rabbit fever I'm sure you know about. I'm sure, too, that you know something about Gruinard Island; that will become inhabitable again in a few decades. But have they told you everything? 'Purple Possum' for instance? My experiments for the government of this country went far beyond that, indeed at times they went beyond certain Conventions, with a capital 'C'. I did as my government asked, and I did it for my country, but you need to know that if disturbed recklessly those 'substances' could leave a large part of the south coast uninhabitable." The old man paused for breath, then looked Sir Robert straight in the eye.

"I have served my country faithfully and had scant reward for it. I can't expect to be in the New Year's Honours List for things the government can't admit to, but under the circumstances I am entitled to make some demands." Sir Robert did not demur. "So, by twelve noon tomorrow you will have arranged these things. One – my daughter and her cousins are to be released, and through appropriate channels it will be made known that they are blameless. Which they are, obviously. Two – the substances will be safely removed and disposed of in accordance with my previous requests and with immediate effect. Some semi-digestible story can be created – that's what you chaps do. Three – I think you know what that is – our mutual interest in keeping this completely secret."

Sir Robert could not quite return the professor's gimlet stare. He coughed.

"Professor Kirrin, I understand your personal interest in this matter and I assure you that we will do our best to resolve this in a manner that is satisfactory to all concerned. This is, however, a matter of national security, and..."

"Indeed? I've heard that before, Sir Robert. It is my terms in full or nothing. Knowing how devious shape-shifters in government work I have given myself a little protection – a Doomsday Machine you might call it. Oh, for goodness sake don't look for your panic button. It doesn't devastate cities or citizens. Its effects are powerful, however, in destroying the cosy complacency of those civil servants who think their own comfort trumps the safety of our country. I am a scientist. I have kept notes of all my activities on government projects, and that means the legal and the – how shall I put it? – the un-conventional. Would that be the word, Sir Robert? The Doomsday part is, shall we say, a timely arrangement. I have lodged my notes with a publisher abroad, who has them typeset and ready to print by twelve noon GMT tomorrow unless they get a telegram from me telling them not to."

The normally phlegmatic features of the Cabinet Secretary became pale and he stood up.

"That's blackmail!"

"I am helping you to do the right thing Sir Robert. The safe and decent thing. And to keep it quiet."

"You are asking me to be economical with the truth?"

"I'm asking you lie for your country."

There was a long pause.

"So, will you speak with the Prime Minister now?" asked the Professor, only it wasn't a question. He was leaning on his cane now, but his voice did not waver.

"I don't think that will be necessary," the Cabinet Secretary replied. "I'm sure everything will all be arranged as you wish."

37

A Very Important Cabinet Office Briefing

"So, what does all that mean?" asked a young, pink-cheeked researcher as he filed the minutes of the cabinet meeting. His older companion grinned.

"They've messed up! Government were lax about a load of chemicals they got some scientist to use on some island. Didn't sort out the residues, like they planned. It got forgotten. Only somehow it all got found by the Drugs Squad after some sort of mistake, and a load of people got arrested."

"Oh, *them!*"

"Yep – *them*. Seems they were banged up when they didn't have a clue about the stuff. One of them was done for a Tupperware tub of scouring powder, can you believe! Like to have seen someone snorting that!"

The pink-cheeked one grinned. "What will happen now?"

"They'll be released, get a hushed-up apology and probably some hush money, and Margaret will bury whole thing. Seems the scientist chap did some properly good work and the government got egg on its face. The stuff gets removed pronto. So, keep schtum, OK?"

38

Just Like Old Times!

"Gentlemen, welcome back to Kirrin," said the Chief Constable to the re-assembled day-trippers from Fleet Street who had been rounded up and bussed back to The Kirrin Arms. "I must apologise for the delay and any inconvenience but I am pleased to say you can now publish the story which you have been waiting for. The story that is being handed round in the press release. *That* is your story – nothing else." The Chief Constable wondered if he had put enough emphasis on the word. He nodded theatrically towards the Brigadier who stood silently at the back of the room.

"And I am delighted to welcome back to Kirrin the people who are sitting here with me. Mr. Julian Kirrin, his brother Sgt. Richard Kirrin, his sister Mrs. Anne Stonehouse, and his cousin, Miss Georgi..." he stopped himself just in time, "Ms. George Kirrin and, er, her dog. They are, I need not remind you, *old* friends of the county constabulary. We all know about the plots and ne'er-do-wells they exposed as youngsters. I'm very pleased to tell you that their sleuthing skills have not deserted them. They have, in the last few days, been helping with our enquiries in a very real sense. Indeed, to that end they have been pretending to be suspects themselves, and to go deep undercover in prison. I must stress they have done *nothing wrong*. We are very grateful for their crime fighting efforts once again. I don't know what we would have done without them. I only regret that this is so important and so secret that for reasons of national security I cannot tell you more."

He paused, and again nodded seriously towards the Brigadier who remained impassive at the back of the room.

"Everything is in the press release. It only remains for me to publicly thank them all, and give them these medals, which have been produced specially." The Kirrins formed a line like Prize Day at school.

"Mr. Kirrin!" He shook Julian's hand with exaggerated heartiness.

"Sgt. Kirrin!" He was even more vigorous.

"Dear lady!" He kissed Anne on the cheek.

"…and Ms. Kirrin!" He started to lean forward but checked himself and held out his hand. As the group posed for the photograph he thought it had gone off pretty well. He still had a few disgruntled officers to square off, but the promise of a knighthood in the New Year's Honours List would please the lady wife. The cameras flashed, and they all blinked.

39

Plenty to Say!

The public bar of The Kirrin Arms had never been so full. A huge buffet was laid out on a long table at the end of the room, and the banner above it, painted by the twins onto a large bed-sheet, read *Wellcome Back to Kirrin!* in vivid and rather lumpy powder-paint colours. At the other end of the room bottles of wine and jugs of orange squash and ginger beer were already leaving sticky coloured rings on the white cloth as glasses were filled and refilled. The air was alive with noisy chatter and movement, and the sausage rolls had already attracted a cluster of children. The chairs and tables which sat sociably around the rest of the room were overflowing. Most of the village had turned out, many of them dressed up smartly for the occasion, and a couple of reporters had sneaked in. Mostly, though, the place was buzzing with Kirrins.

Julian, well turned out as ever, stood in the centre of the room in a grey suit sipping at a huge glass of wine and talking about layers of power in British prisons and the trading of basic commodities. He had one arm through Bianca's who was nodding in glossy agreement, every now and then casting her eye across to the table nearest the door to the pub office. Hugh was sitting there, leaning towards Quentin and Yu Na, deep in earnest conversation.

"Forty minutes should do it," said Hugh. He glanced around and lowered his voice further. "Father has his speech timed for two-thirty, which is ten minutes away. Radclyffe has everything ready for when we leave the locals to it. I tell you, Uncle Quentin, I'm pretty excited, but we have to keep schtum about the details until the locals have trotted off. Can't risk you being the next one to sample porridge every morning."

"Good God, no. And what would Yu Na do without me to keep her feet warm?" said the old man, drily. Yu Na smiled and firmly dabbed a crumb of pastry off his mouth. Perhaps she was the attentive helpmeet Anne had envisioned for her uncle after all.

Anne herself was hovering beside Aunt Fanny and beaming round at the gathering. Rupert hadn't managed to make it today, but she found she was really almost glad. He wouldn't have enjoyed it *at all*. George had shared a cup of coffee with Anne earlier in the day and said a few things about Rupert and his husbandly ways which had a habit of popping into Anne's mind unbidden every now and again. She would jolly well think about them, too!

There was George, a glass of beer in her hand, explaining to an open-mouthed Joan just what went on at a Women's Empowerment meeting, and how she had got a strong group going at Holloway, which she would continue to visit as much as she could. It had been truly awful to be locked up, but George had met some really interesting people. Really strong.

Joan was enjoying the whole thing thoroughly. The coast-guard, sitting to her left as usual, was waving his pipe grumpily and trying to get her to fetch him some more pickled onions. Well, thought Joan, she didn't always have to be at anyone's beck and call, and the odd please and thank-you wouldn't go amiss. She stopped the pipe-waving with a quick *v's-up* in its direction, opened her mouth in shock at her own gesture, then burst into wobbly laughter. George clapped her on the back.

Gary, chomping crumbs under the buffet table, had been remarkably well behaved, though he toddled through everyone's legs to the office door and sniffed it every now and then before the lure of the sausage rolls drew him back. Radclyffe was here one minute and gone the next, so not much had changed there.

Anne, sitting with Aunt Fanny, shifted her focus to the twins. Julie was sharing a plateful of cheesy pineapple sticks with Leanne and Susan, the three of them sitting on the floor in the corner and reading out the Cathy and Claire letters from last Thursday's *Jackie* Magazine. They were spluttering with laughter, and oblivious to everyone else. Leanne and Susan were from the village, and Julie had struck up a lively friendship with them. Anne could see her daughter's sulky look give way to a relaxed giggle quite often these days, mostly when they were here at Kirrin. Thank goodness the separation from her mother for those three dreadful days had not seemed to have done any permanent damage.

Against the end wall, Jonny stood watching intently. He held a large sketchbook and was carefully drawing the tables and chairs, food and drink, windows, doors, banner and clusters of people, young and old, in minute detail, frowning in concentration and stopping to sharpen his pencil every minute or so. He had left his transistor radio at home. Hugh, leaving Quentin and Yu Na for a moment, wandered across and took a look over Jonny's shoulder. The boy was quite talented! Anne, glancing up, caught his eye and looked proud.

Dick was standing at the buffet table resisting a third sausage roll quite heroically. The prison diet had been disgusting, but he had managed to shape up quite a bit.

"Well, now, Dick Kirrin, we want to be making the most of

our time, now don't we?" whispered a lilting voice. "And I've got a job you could help me with. Can't do it on my own." Jo had crept up behind Dick and was on tiptoes, tickling his ear with her breath, almost making him spill his glass of Watneys. She was wearing a very sassy pair of Doc Marten boots with a black skirt and a red and black striped sweater that reminded him of Minnie the Minx. She didn't dress remotely like anyone else he knew, and Dick thought she was beautiful. He closed his eyes briefly as she slipped her hand into his and led him away from the chatter and into the pub kitchen. The one with the noisy dishwashing machine.

Back in the main room the cheerful crowd fell silent as Julian tapped his glass several times with a spoon.

"Ladies, gentlemen, children, and especially Kirrins," he began. "We, that is my brother Dick, my sister Anne and my cousin George, want to thank you for standing by us over the last few months which have been a difficult time for all of us. We hope you missed us. We certainly missed you while we were away on our little 'holiday'. We met some new friends while were were locked up, but none of them will replace our good old friends in Kirrin."

Cheers and raised glasses went round the room.

"I know there have been lots of rumours, and for very good reasons I can't tell you the whole story. However, if any of you think this has something to do with my uncle Quentin and things that are TOP SECRET and of great help to our country I won't say you are wrong. The important thing is that it's over now. Kirrin Island is perfectly safe, as those of you know who have been shown around by our young guides, my son Hugh and my nephew Radclyffe. And thank you for welcoming Radclyffe (and Gary, of course) into the Kirrin community; I know my nephew finds it very different from London but he hasn't scared the fish away and I'm sure he'll learn to drive the launch a little more slowly!" Julian looked around for Radclyffe who was sitting at the bar with two of Kirrin's grizzled fishermen, Gary at his feet. They raised their glasses to the assembly and the villagers laughed and clapped. Julian's heart warmed to all of them, and he found this somewhat new feeling very agreeable.

"And because Kirrin is such a lovely place, you are going to be seeing more of us. Young Hugh here will be running this end of Kirrin Enterprises. We have finalised the investment required to complete Phase II, which means lots more local jobs for you and for your children, to keep the tourists rolling in. Kirrin is on the map!

"My brother Dick says he has had enough of pounding the beat in London and I am pleased – very pleased – to say that in future he'll be pulling the pints as landlord here at The Kirrin Arms." Julian looked around for Dick, but couldn't see him anywhere. "Er, yes – here at The Kirrin Arms with staunch help from the delightful Jo." He couldn't see her either. Never mind. Shouts of approval went up, along with a few suggesting free drinks might be just the thing. Julian took another mouthful of wine and continued.

"You've also welcomed my little nephew and niece while they have been spending weekends with their Aunt Fanny. I hope they haven't become Kirrin rascals while they've been here. If they haven't learned Kirrin ways yet, they will have plenty of time to do so. A little bird tells me that Kirrin Cottage may soon be seeing a lot more of them and their mother." Polite cheers and clapping rippled round.

"And finally, I've agreed something rather special with my cousin George. Outside the high season she will have Kirrin

Island entirely at her own disposal. She has plans to use it for some of her groups from London, those who need refuge and relaxation and fresh air. This is splendid, and means you'll have trade all year round. Now I know some of these Londoners have green hair, tattoos and bits of metal sticking through strange places, but George has introduced me to a few and I can assure you all they don't bite!" Julian wasn't quite as confident about that as he sounded, but it got a laugh, and even a smile from George. George's motley crew hadn't been as difficult as he had feared, and the village had a few punk rockers and even the odd feminist of its own these days. Perhaps George had mellowed, and perhaps he had too.

"So, good folk of Kirrin, thank you all. We have a little family matter to attend to, so we are going to slip out to The Smugglers' Bar in a moment. But you don't have to go. I heard some shouting at the back. I'm sure I heard your voice Mr. Coastguard, and as a way of showing our thanks to you all the bar will remain open for half an hour more. Enjoy yourselves, and don't fall off the quay on your way home, because there are free drinks for everybody!" Tumultuous applause greeted this last announcement, and shouts of *For he's a jolly good fellow.*

The mood was jolly, and the villagers began to chatter and comment to each other while crowding around the bar, which was staffed by two cheerful locals.

Hugh slipped quickly over to the door connecting the public bar to The Smugglers' and unlocked it. His father and Bianca followed him quickly and within minutes Quentin, Yu Na, and all of the Kirrins had joined them, hustled through by an insistent Hugh, who locked the door from the inside as soon as everyone was through. He and Radclyffe looked distinctly excited. The place was calm enough for Anne to hiccup gently and for the extended family members to gather around the largest table, shuffled there by Julian, who was behaving rather mysteriously. Once everyone had settled, Jo and Dick reappeared from the kitchen door with cups of coffee on trays, looking rather dishevelled, Anne thought. She looked a bit confused as Hugh disappeared through the office door with a nod at his father, but paid attention as Julian stood up at the head of the table and cleared his throat again. Quentin looked at him with an air of self-importance which George found irritating. What was going on now? Another speech, presumably. And why was Yu Na, of all people, taking Gary outside? He wasn't being sick at the moment as far as she could tell.

"Here we are. The family together again." George looked a little pointedly at Bianca but Julian ignored her. "We have learned a lot of tough things and, er, I think I can safely say that we have come through yet another adventure together and triumphed! But we are not quite together. Not all of us. All summer there has been someone missing, someone who should have been at our sides, sharing our troubles and our joys." There was a respectful silence as he continued. "However, Uncle Quentin" (here he turned to the old man, who was frowning thoughtfully) "is not a world-renowned scientist for nothing. He and Yu Na's father, himself a remarkable scientist in his field, have been hard at work for several months, both in Korea and, more recently, in England. They have achieved a special and most important piece of work – yes, very Top Secret work – which we would now like to share with you all. Please stay very quiet now, while we show you something truly magical."

There was a proper silence – the first of the day – while the Kirrins held their breath, Anne with an arm around each twin. All heads turned as the door to the pub office opened slowly and through it, black nose first, came pattering a glorious jumble of a puppy, tongue hanging out, with a lopsided grinning expression on his silky face. He stopped and sniffed the pub smells for a second, wagged his plumy tail, then trotted over to George, who was sitting stock still, her eyes, blue and direct, shining wetly at the corners. The creature put his front paws up on her lap and rested his chin against her knees, his brown eyes looking up at hers.

"Timmy," whispered George, her hand gently on his head. "Timmy, is it you?"

"Alright, Gary?" enquired Radclyffe outside in the car park. "Don't worry, mate. I'll still hang out with you. It's getting a bit cold. Let's go for a run."

He untied Gary, who seemed indifferent to the suggestion, and the pair of them set off along the quay at a trot. Radclyffe's thoughts, as he looked across the bay to Kirrin Island, were confusing him. This animal copying business – *cloning*, his grandfather had called it – was weird and exciting, and he'd been part of the conspiracy, trusted by Hugh.

Hugh had told him all about it. This Timmy copying idea had begun when Quentin had met Yu Na's father at a conference in Korea and found out what the man was doing. With Julian's money, Yu Na's father had promised to produce a genuine copy – or *clone* – of his mother's old dog, and claimed to have succeeded through the use of some old hairs and a tooth salvaged from the manky old basket Aunt Fanny still had hanging around the cottage. Could they do that? It was like some sci-fi movie, only film writers wouldn't have wasted all the effort on a dog. They would have done a dinosaur or something.

Radclyffe stopped running for a few seconds and looked

down at his feet. How had he come into being himself? His mother had never talked about it, never told him anything about a father, shutting him up if he tried to find out. He decided there and then to ask her again. It was a good time, he had never seen her so happy as when she had been introduced to the new Timmy.

Yu Na, helping her husband with his toenails that evening, looked quizzical.

"Quentin, what do you say about my father? He is a very naughty man, no? Many men in the laboratories are naughty. They think you are in love with them and they annoy you. So many times they annoy me when I assist my father at his work. You did not do this, Quentin. You see that I have the brains in my head, and so here we are."

"Indeed, here we are, my little lab-coat genius," said Quentin, as he watched her fold his socks and place a glass by the bed for his teeth. The irony didn't strike either of them.

"My father, though, is different," continued Yu Na. He is a proud and ambitious man. That little dog – you know, Quentin, he is not coming from the Timmy DNA cells. My father is telling all the people that he can do this thing, and yet I think he is finding it too difficult. This little dog, maybe, is found by my father's people because he is looking like the special dog. He sent it to you at Kirrin, all very secret and special, and everybody thinks this is very good science."

Quentin looked at her wryly for a moment, then barked out a short laugh.

"Ha! You really might be right, my dear. You really might. But I don't think we will say anything to Julian, do you?"

40

Anne Has Lots of Fun!

November 1979

The kitchen at Kirrin Cottage smelled of hot, fresh scones and Anne hummed along to the radio. *Hooray, hooray! It's a holi-holiday!*

It was a funny song to be popular when the evenings were drawing in, thought Anne, but she rather liked it nevertheless. She popped a couple of scones on a plate, split them open and added generous dollops of butter and raspberry jam. In the corner Aunt Fanny beamed, cosy in a rather startling turquoise poncho chosen for her by Julie. A cup of cocoa with a tiny splash of warming brandy, her ration for the day, steamed gently on the side table next to her armchair, but she seemed in no hurry to finish it.

"Here you are, Aunt Fanny. Scones are best eaten straight from the oven, aren't they?" Anne sat next to her aunt, and the two women munched contentedly. The kitchen was gleaming, and looked so pretty now Anne had arranged all the china on the dresser. It wasn't in the least bit fashionable, but it felt real and permanent. It was already getting dark, and Anne enjoyed the glow of the fire on her face. Jonny and Julie would be home from school soon, and would devour the rest of the scones. Julie might bring her friend Leanne back, and they would all want to wrap up warmly and play outside in the dark for a little while before tea.

Life in Wimbledon somehow seemed very grey in comparison to life now. Rupert belonged in the grey offices and helpful (though certainly not grey) Miss Perkins was welcome to him. Perhaps she appreciated being the little woman with the hostess trolley, but Anne didn't miss it at all. She wondered for a minute about herself, her life. She hadn't turned into George – she still *liked* looking after everyone, and making everywhere cosy – but it was different now. She had been listening to Jenni Murray on Radio 4, who was rather wonderful. Now she was pleasing herself.

Anne thought about her twins, walking home from the village school together. When she had made her plans to leave Rupert, move to Kirrin Cottage and care for Aunt Fanny, her main worry had been the twins' school. Anne visited the tiny village primary school in Kirrin. The headmistress had been so wise and kind, and not at all alarmed by Jonny's unusual behaviour.

"Bless him – he needs a bit of time to relax," Mrs. Bloom had said. "We're not all cut from the same cloth, and a good thing too. You let the twins spend a year with us before they move on to the seniors. It won't hurt holding back a year. Julie can make friends and Jonny can find out what he's really good at. There's plenty of time for worrying when they're older."

And she had been right. So far, the twins were enjoying village life more than she could have imagined, and the grimy weeks of Holloway Prison were receding into a tidily tucked away corner of Anne's memory. Julie's friend, Leanne, who wasn't much like any of the girls at her last school, was inclined to invent mad games with torches, garden tables and old sheets, and the garden at Kirrin was proving just the place for trying them out. And Jonny. Well, he hadn't exactly got a *friend* as such, but the tight grip on his pocket radio and his plastic shark had loosened, and he was developing a talent for drawing which absorbed him and delighted Anne. His classmates were in the habit of asking him to draw cartoons of Scooby Doo and The Pink Panther, and he obliged with serious concentration. He was inclined to observe Julie and Leanne building their tent-like structures, and sometimes crawled inside to share the plates of squishy cheese triangles which they squeezed from little holes in the foil, giggling as the creamy snakes appeared. Last Saturday he had taken a trip to the Dorchester Woolworths with Dick and Jo, and was cautiously eyeing up a skateboard. He seemed contented.

It's a holi-holiday! Bony M finished their song and Anne smiled. This wasn't a holiday – this was real life. She shouldn't really be sitting around – she had a Tupperware Party to plan, and invitations to write to all the village mothers – but the moment felt precious. She caught Aunt Fanny's eye, and the old lady twinkled back. Without a word, Anne rose and poured herself a cup of cocoa, settling back into her seat. The two women raised their china and sipped.

41

Julian Does Some Thinking

Julian Kirrin loosened his collar a little, and leaned back in his leather chair. The tumbler beside him was nearly empty, the Newton's Cradle had stopped clicking, and he was mellow. Bianca would be here soon and they would walk out along the South Bank for a meal. Life was good.

The last few months had been eventful, but everything was turning out rather splendidly. It hadn't looked like that when he had been arrested – far from it. He'd been stupid taking that tiny pinch of cocaine to Kirrin; it wasn't a habit, other than a lazy one. It was part of the culture in the city with friends. He'd learned a lesson from that – he'd stick to Chivas Regal in future.

Prison was not something he wanted to repeat. He'd kept his head down, but the noise and smell would stay with him forever. Clanging metal, shouting all night, the sweat and smell of men in confined spaces. And slopping out. Charm and old boy networks made no impact on that.

As a child Julian had sometimes wondered whether all that stuff Quentin used to say about doing top secret work for the government had just been an excuse to stop the children bothering him. He knew, now, that it was all true, even if they still didn't know exactly what Quentin had done all those years ago. His uncle clearly had respect in the highest places. He had come up trumps there, and he had come up with the goods too: the dog. Now *that* had been a coup. Truly he was a remarkable scientist.

A flicker of regret went through Julian's business brain. Had he let an opportunity slip through his hands? There must be a market for cloning pets – all those families and rich old women grieving dead dogs and lost cats. Was there a future in, what would you call it, *clonology*? No, science wasn't his thing. He would leave it with Quentin and his Korean partners. Knowing his uncle, he wouldn't do anything with it. Typical, thought Julian. We British invent something and then someone else makes money out of it. Six months ago that would have troubled him – he had mellowed.

He looked across at the table by the window, the model of Kirrin Island with all his developments completed to scale, looking more and more real as dark shadows formed from the sun setting over London. Phase II was well underway now that funding had been secured. He hadn't said anything to deter the rumours that he had connections at the highest levels; investors liked that.

That was enough for now. Making money was all well and good, but he had other priorities. He picked up the little box marked Cartier from the table and opened it. Yes, he thought, Bianca will like that. The diamond was big enough to be impressive but not too ostentatious.

The intercom buzzed. Julian got up, slipped the box into the pocket of his jacket, checked his hair at the reflection in the big window and went to open the door.

42

Dick Has a Super Day!

Julian had made a pretty good job of The Kirrin Arms. All it needed now was a better selection of Real Ale, a lick of paint in the public bar and a climbing frame outside for the kiddies. Jo would soon have everything sorted out. Running the pub with her was nothing short of amazing, and he was the luckiest man alive, ever. Jo could change barrels, deal with breweries, keep the accounts and make a jolly good hotpot.

He, Dick, was able to use his skills to cheer up the locals on a dark November evening like this one, and clear out those who had had more than was good for them. Actually, Jo could probably do that, too, but she let him keep order in his own way.

The new mystery of Kirrin Island had proved a godsend to the takings, and Dick was not ashamed to bask in a bit of glory and tell stories of his interesting past to admiring tourists.

Anne and the twins were round the corner in Kirrin Cottage, and he enjoyed being their uncle now Anne was more relaxed. So much so, that Jo had suggested forty-one wasn't *necessarily* past it when it came to babies. That had made Dick grin more than ever.

George was here much of the time, now she had plans for the island, too. She was still a strange one. Having spent most of her childhood encounters scrapping furiously with Jo, the two were (most of the time) close friends. Sometimes, though, Dick thought George looked at him a bit strangely. Could she be just a tiny tad jealous of him? Jo was so very lovely, but it was a boyish kind of lovely. He wasn't in any doubt about Jo, of course, but even so, he would have to hold on to her tight.

Dick didn't miss life in uniform. He could still be useful to the police, and often was, but swarthy men in Astrakhan collars would always be welcome guests at The Kirrin Arms.

At the bar, Jo pulled the beer lever towards her and a pint of Smuggler's Ale streamed smoothly into the glass. She handed it over to a sturdy man in a much-worn Guernsey sweater.

"Here you are, James. I hear George likes the work you did on her boat. Smashing job, she said. Like you used to do when she was a kid."

"Not bad." James grinned as he took the glass over to the old coastguard who glared around at everyone before gulping deeply and smacking his lips. James sat down and grinned again.

"George liked her boat right enough," he said to the coastguard. "Pretty stupid idea, patching and painting that old wooden thing when she could have had a new fibreglass model instead. Still, if that's what Mr. Julian ordered, who am I to argue? It's all money in my wallet. She liked it, anyway. Always did." He looked quite soft, though, when he spoke of George. He spoke of her a lot, too. Jo wondered how that might end? James was handsome and sensible. It had possibilities, she thought.

The coastguard wiped the foam from his mouth and nodded.

"They'll do, I suppose. The Kirrin lot, I mean. My grandson'll do OK with fishing trips for the extra visitors once the place is up and running in the spring. Joan's alright, too – she's going to do a bit of work over there at bank holidays – having her photo took with the scones or something."

Jo looked around the room. There was talk and laughter, and

there, sitting at a table with a couple of lads, was Dick telling one of his jokes; the laughing ex-policeman. The lads were laughing too. Jo smiled. Dick was in his element as landlord of The Kirrin.

"Dick," called Jo. "I don't want to spoil your evening, but we got a barrel needs changing. Think you could tear yourself away?" Within a second Dick was at her side, his face lit up with pleasure. "Only you see," Jo put her mouth close to his ear, "I wouldn't want to be doing it in my condition…"

Dick stood absolutely still for a moment. His mouth opened.

"Your condition? You mean…are you…are we…are we going to…?" he whispered. She nodded, an amused smile on her face.

"Looks like I'll be accepting that proposal of marriage quite sharpish!"

With a whoop, he lifted Jo off her feet and twirled her round the bar and into the crowd, almost falling over his own feet before setting her down in a chair and placing her feet carefully on a rather sticky table. Jo nudged him.

"Go on, then – they're all watching. Tell them, if you like! I don't care if they don't approve. Never was one for doing things the right way round."

Dick sprung to his feet and stood just behind Jo, one arm protectively on her shoulder. He beamed around at the audience of expectant faces.

"Wow!" he said. "Um – wow! Jo's going to marry me and we're going to have a…a…well, actually a baby! A baby! It's a free drink for everyone.

A cheer rose up around them as Dick kissed Jo, then tripped over her feet as he rushed to the bar to fill the waving glasses.

43

George Has a Wonderful Time!

As George got into her boat and pushed it away she sighed with pleasure. She slipped her hands into the oars, beautifully varnished, and admired the fresh green and red paint. James had done a wonderful job, and Julian must have paid him well. She must find her old friend and buy him a drink later. Perhaps he'd come out to the island in it with her, just to try it out – that would be OK. Very nice, actually. The little vessel, which had carried her and her cousins all through their childhood, was as sturdy as new. The puppy in the prow was sitting upright, alert and excited, tail wagging. The sea was quite choppy, but George knew she could handle it.

"Jimmy," she whispered, "we are going back to our island – just you and me – for a little while."

She soon reached a steady rhythm, and bobbed her way round the wreck and its rocks and into the little harbour. Jimmy was quick to jump out onto the beach, and ran around her ankles excitedly. Together the pair walked past the Portakabin and up towards the castle, which nestled quietly under the sky, enjoying a rest from the renovations in the late November sunshine. She didn't go inside, but sat for a while with her back resting against its strong grey walls, her hand tousling the pup's head.

Her castle would be alright. It wasn't everything she wanted, and she had had to accept that, but for at least two months of the year – every March and every October – it would be hers entirely, a place where she could bring those who needed its comforting walls and its guardian waters. There were plenty of people who she could share it with – women who were victims, women who needed respite, sometimes with their children. That would be a fine thing. And sometimes she would come alone, because that was a fine thing too.

She thought about Radclyffe, revelling in his job as driver of the Pride of Kirrin. He had discovered a love of the sea like his mother's, and had astonished her with his ready move to the village, accepting a tiny room at the pub, washing up when needed, and leaving school for good. He was so relaxed. He would make his way as part of the family business, and George didn't mind that. He would be alright. Even Gary seemed to have settled down, and rarely left the boy's side.

She looked down at Jimmy. His tongue hung out of his mouth, licking her hand now and again, and his soft head on her lap was so like the one she had longed for. He wasn't Tim, though, and no dog ever could be. Whatever Julian and the others believed, he wasn't Timmy's clone either. There were too many little differences – tiny ones, like his ear shape – for George to believe that the scientists had come up with a genuine replica of Timmy. So Julian had been deceived. Timmy was unique, and always would be. But this was Jimmy, and he was a fine dog.

For the first time in many years, George realised that she was happy. She and Jim stood up and walked down the hill towards the setting sun, rabbits scattering before them. The little dog pricked his ears up and barked excitedly.

"Jimmy," said George. "Don't you dare!"

Afterword

Surely that didn't happen?

Were you alive in 1979? If not some of the things in this book may seem unbelievable. Even if, like us, you were, the memory can play strange tricks. This is a work of fiction, but because it is set in a specific time we've tried to keep our fiction factual.

If you doubt this, or are fascinated by what it was really like, or if you just want to show your children, we have a Facebook page on which we have posted some of our background material. This includes things we didn't use, and other material from the period. Some of it is funny, though not all of it was funny at the time. We hope you will enjoy it with same joy, horror and embarrassment that we did.

- What was a Filofax?
- What was wrong with telephones?
- Why did policemen grow their hair long for Operation Julie?
- Were young policeman told to be suspicious of unpolished shoes?
- How did Radclyffe get his name?
- Was there any cloning going on in 1979?
- Why was Anne excited about Tupperware?

- What was the best Ford Capri you could get?
- What fabulous fashions, records and gadgets were on offer?

If you want to share your memories or tell us we've got something wrong join us on our Facebook page: www.facebook.com/returntokirrin

Neil and Suzy

Book Clubs: Ideas for Discussion

- Which character did you want to be when you were a child? Why? Would you change your mind now?
- Many libraries, and some parents, banned Enid Blyton during the 1960s and 1970s, for either literary or idealistic reasons. Were you encouraged to read the original stories as a child? If not, why not? Do you think that guidance was justified? Would you encourage your own children to read the stories now?
- Which character has the most freedom? And the least? Did you have the same freedom as the characters?
- Discuss the gender stereotypes and attitudes to race and class which some of the 1979 characters show. If you read the original stories, how do these compare? And how have things changed since 1979?
- Has childhood changed fundamentally? In what ways were children more or less independent and resourceful in 1950s? 1979? 2017? Are your ideas about this based on fiction or reality?
- Joan suggests that Julian might have been dishonest over some small change in the village shop once, as a child. This seems unlikely, given his strict attitude to the truth at the time, but might Joan be right?

- Do you recognise any of the parenting styles?
- Will Jonny be alright?

Special Thanks

We should start with our parents who introduced us to stories, and gave us childhoods with time enough to read them. Then our daughter Lucy, for encouragement, re-typing the manuscript lost to an IT upgrade, and her perceptive notes; our son George, for believing his parents capable of doing something creative; our friends Caroline M, Polly L and Nikki L (lovely ladies all, who have laughed at the funny bits, and given invaluable feedback), Caroline S (timeline genius), the always encouraging Frome Writers' Bootcamp members, Frome Writers' Collective, The Alliance of Independent Authors, SilverWood Books, and Mark Lloyd of onfirecreative.co.uk for his fabulous cover design. Above all, we take our hats off to Enid Blyton herself. Her original stories about Julian, Dick, Anne, George and Timmy are still delighting children today, which makes us smile.

Frome, August 2017

Lightning Source UK Ltd.
Milton Keynes UK
UKOW04f1702281017
311777UK00002B/42/P